CRONIN'S KEY II

N.R. WALKER

COPYRIGHT

Cover Artist: Sara York
Editor: Boho Edits
Cronin's Key © 2015 N.R. Walker
Second Edition 2017

All Rights Reserved:

Warning

Intended for an 18+ audience only. This book contains material that maybe offensive to some and is intended for a mature, adult audience. It contains graphic language, explicit sexual content, and adult situations.

Trademark Acknowledgements:

The Omen: 1976 Film, 20th Century Fox.

Patek Philippe: Patek Philippe SA

YouTube: Google Inc.,

iPad: Apple Inc.,

My Little Pony: Hasbro, Inc.

Google: Google, Inc.,

Xanax: Pfizer Inc.,

Thor (in context used): Marvel Entertainment LLC (Walt Disney Company)

Happy Gilmore: Universal Studios Inc.

Author acknowledgement:

The spelling of the word Terracotta is taken from The Qin Tomb Terracotta Warriors and Horses Museum.
http://www.chinahighlights.com/xian/terracotta-army/

DEDICATION

For my readers. Without you, my words would seem impossible.

CRONIN'S KEY II

N.R. WALKER

CHAPTER ONE

ALEC SAT on the sofa with his feet on the coffee table reading the *New York Times* on an iPad. He'd look up every so often at the apartment, at Cronin's walls of memorabilia, smiling at the antiques shelved there, then at the vampire beside him.

"What's so funny?" Cronin asked. He didn't even look up from the Chinese newspaper he was reading, though a smile played at his lips.

"I was just looking over all your relics," Alec explained. Cronin had told him about most of the artifacts he'd collected, and despite their conversations starting with good intentions, they usually ended up in the bedroom. Or on the sofa, or on the floor, or over the dining table. "I mean, those antiques are pretty cool, but you're my favorite."

Cronin looked up at Alec then. "Your favorite antique?"

"Well." Alec's grin widened. "You are a 744 vintage. I think you qualify."

Cronin smiled, amused. "And you're a what?"

Alec imitated the guy from Antiques Roadshow. "A

contemporary piece, 1980s Americana. Perfect condition, well-endowed."

Cronin laughed at that. "You're bored."

"Ugh." Alec groaned and let his head fall back on the sofa. "*So* bored."

He'd spent the last eight weeks holed up in Cronin's lavish New York City apartment. His days, which were now fully nighttime hours, consisted of a workout regime—Cronin had installed gym equipment in the cinema room to curb Alec's boredom—hours of foreplay and sex, the occasional movie on Netflix, and reading and researching vampire histories. He rarely left the apartment.

The view was spectacular, and if he wanted something —anything—he could simply order it, pay for it with Cronin's black credit card, and have it delivered. But he was still confined to quarters. Meaning he was still wanted by NYPD, his former colleagues no less, though the hype had died down.

The fact that his and Cronin's disappearing acts, which had been caught on CCTV—once in his department's office area and once in the department's stores facility—had been leaked on YouTube, meant Alec's relatively quiet and unnoticed disappearance had gone global.

The footage went viral, making news headlines around the world and him an internet sensation. Some called it a hoax and disregarded what was just too impossible to understand, and others called it what it was.

Quantum leaping.

Cronin's ability to appear anywhere in the world—or *leaping* as they called it—was, in Alec's opinion, the best talent a vampire could have. And it *was* awesome. Not that they really went anywhere these last eight weeks.

It still wasn't a great idea for Alec to be seen in public,

and Cronin couldn't go out in the sunlight. That limited their outings to faraway places, wherever it was night.

Alec sighed and went over to the shelves lined with Cronin's memorabilia. He had wanted to know about all the items Cronin thought important enough to collect over the last twelve hundred years. As a vampire, Cronin had seen things Alec couldn't begin to imagine, and he wanted to know as much as he could. He'd asked about most of them, but went to one display that held three items he'd not gotten to yet. Alec put his hand out, almost touching the artifact. "Can I touch it?"

Cronin now stood beside him. "Of course," he answered with a smile.

Alec carefully picked up the small, crudely glazed bottle, admiring it as he turned it in his hands. It was whitish-brown and looked like a child had made it in school art class. "What about this one?"

"That is a Mayan poison bottle."

Alec blinked. "Oh." He changed how he was holding it, as though it would now bite.

Cronin smiled. "The year was 821. Jodis and I went there and were ill-received. Can't imagine why."

Alec laughed and rolled his eyes. "No, I can't imagine why either."

"A witch-doctor offered us a drink," Cronin said, nodding toward the bottle. "Courteous fellow."

"Well, it would have been rude to refuse," Alec added sarcastically.

"Yes, quite." Cronin said, amused. "In the end, he drank it himself rather than see his end with one of us."

"And this one?" Alec picked up what looked like a bone knife.

"Ah, that's a Peruvian weaver's bone wand."

"Of course it is."

Cronin chuckled. "It's from 1288. An old woman stabbed me with it."

Alec's mouth fell open. "She what?"

"She stabbed me, only barely." Cronin was still smiling. "Eiji and Jodis thought it funny that an elderly human woman could do such a thing. She was no taller than four foot."

"I hope you killed her."

Cronin barked out a laugh. "Uh, no. Her heart gave out before I had the chance."

Alec turned back to the shelves and picked up a long metal pin with a jeweled end. It looked expensive. "And this?"

"That is a seventeenth century French shawl pin," Cronin said, almost wistfully. "A man tried to stab me with it. I believe it belonged to his wife."

"What is it with you and being stabbed?"

Cronin sniffed indignantly. "It must be my charming personality."

Alec snorted. "If by charming personality you mean vampire about to kill them, then yes, I think so too." But the truth was, Alec knew from years of police work that stabbing was an intimate crime; the offender was well within the other person's personal space. He frowned. "I don't like the idea of you being close enough to bite someone else. Or that you have your mouth on their skin... or your teeth."

Cronin took the shawl pin from Alec and put it back on the shelf. "It doesn't bother you that I kill people, only that I have my lips on them when I bite them?"

Alec looked to the floor and nodded. "You get close, you touch them, you put your lips on them," he said. He knew he was pouting, but he couldn't seem to stop. "It's not fair."

Cronin put his finger under Alec's chin and lifted his face so he could see his eyes. "It is not the same."

"I know," Alec said petulantly. He knew he was being unreasonable. He craned his neck, exposing it to Cronin. Alec knew there were vampire puncture wounds marking his skin, and he loved them. He wore them with pride. "I like it when your lips are on my neck, when you bite me. When you drink from me."

Cronin leaned in and ran his nose along the bite wounds. "Do I not take enough from you?"

"Never," Alec whispered.

Cronin licked the two bruised hole marks, making Alec shiver. "Do I not bite you enough?"

"Never." Alec was getting dizzy with want. He had to remind himself to breathe. He leaned against Cronin, feeling the strength and warmth of him from his thighs to his neck. He was already getting hard. "It will never be enough."

Cronin kissed Alec's neck once more but pulled away. "I can't keep feeding from you. It can't be good for you."

Alec chuckled. "It is *really* good for me."

This time Cronin laughed, a purr rumbled through his chest. "You test my restraint, yet again. Please know, Alec, I'm not opposed to such a notion. Though the hours spent in bed this morning may suggest you need a rest. Just because I can bite you without changing you, doesn't mean you are unaffected."

Alec groaned. They'd found out after the battle in Egypt that Cronin could bite Alec and not change him into a vampire. It opened a whole world of questions, but more than that, it meant they could have sex while Alec was human. And yes, as much as he wanted Cronin to take him, fuck him, and bite him, his human body needed recuperation. The intense sexual pleasure and slight blood loss took its toll when it was for hours at a time. So as much as he didn't like it, he knew Cronin was right.

But Cronin also had a warped sense of time. Living for twelve hundred years would do that, Alec conceded. So while Cronin was patient and content to sit and read or research for hours upon hours, Alec was restless for something else beyond that, some sense of normalcy. He was used to police work, and now he sat around doing a whole lot of nothing. Even though he'd left normal behind the day he'd met Cronin, the vampire he was fated to, he was still a twenty-nine-year-old man. He needed to do something human. He grinned at Cronin. "Come on, let's go out."

Cronin quirked an eyebrow. "Where to?"

"A club somewhere."

"I meant in which city."

"Oh." Alec was thinking some nightclub in the Meat-packing District would do. He didn't think he'd ever get used to being able to leap to any country he chose. He grinned. "Well, it's night time in Europe. I've always wanted to go to London."

Cronin smiled. "I know just the place."

IT TOOK Alec a second to get his bearings. Leaving a warm and well-lit apartment and landing in a cold, dark alley in the time it took to blink was disorienting. He was used to the pain of leaping now. The feeling of being pixelated and shredded at the cellular level was expected, but he knew it was only momentary.

The cold air blasted him regardless, and he shivered

against Cronin. Cronin took his hand and led him down the alley, out onto the street.

Alec noticed the cars first. The steering wheel was on the wrong side of the car, the cars were on the wrong side of the road. He looked down the neon-lit street, hearing the foreign accents around him as they passed Londoners having a night out. It made him grin.

Cronin walked up to a nightclub door, ignoring the waiting line-up of hopefuls. The bouncers gave him a nod, and Cronin pulled Alec through the doors with him. "Known around here, I take it?"

Cronin looked over his shoulder and smiled at him, giving Alec a glimpse of his vampire fangs. "This establishment is owned by a friend."

Okay then. A vampire nightclub. Alec had no clue what he was walking into, yet he felt no fear. He was with Cronin, after all.

Cronin was an elder of the US East Coast, well-known and well-respected. A healthy dose of well feared didn't hurt his reputation either.

The room was packed and pumping, the floor filled with dancers and drinkers. It was dark inside like most nightclubs Alec had been in, but he could still see that most of the people inside were human. They seemed blissfully ignorant of the company they kept. Alec guessed it kept in line with the vampire law of anonymity, though he did wonder how many of these unknowing humans wouldn't see morning.

As if Cronin could read his mind, he leaned in close and whispered over the loud music, "No one can be harmed here. It would bring too much attention to the owners. It is simply a business owned by one of our kind." Cronin pulled back, his dark eyes black, his normally rust colored hair tinted blue from the neon light above. "Drink?"

Alec nodded and Cronin led the way to the bar. Cronin stared for a beat too long at some guy who was leaning against the bar by himself before he nodded and called him by name. "Lars."

Alec wanted to ask what was up with Lars—he was obviously a vampire—but before he had the chance, a voice came from behind them. "Cronin."

Cronin smiled before he'd even turned around. "Kennard."

Alec recognized the man as the elder of the London coven. He'd spoken to him via a video call when they were planning their attack in Egypt two months ago. Kennard was young in human years, no more than twenty. He was shorter than Alec imagined, with a slim build outlined by his fitted jacket with the collar upturned, perfectly styled blond hair, pale skin, and pink lips. He was boyish in looks, but there was a ferociousness lurking under the innocent façade. Alec thought that was what made him even more frightening.

"And Alec!" Kennard said, his eyes lighting up delightedly. He took Alec's hand. "An absolute pleasure to meet you in person."

Cronin made a point of looking at Kennard's hand on Alec's and feigned a snarl. It was hardly menacing, considering he did it with a smile.

"Oh, hush," Kennard waved Cronin off. "You've been hiding him away for weeks now." Kennard smiled up at Alec. Kennard's flair and inflection reminded Alec of an over-acted Shakespeare play, and given Kennard was indeed a London elder, Alec wondered how far wrong he was on when exactly Kennard was human. "So, the hero of

Egypt? No wonder you're fated to Cronin. Only someone rather remarkable would be a match for him."

Alec wasn't sure what to make of Kennard. "Um...."

Cronin laughed and took Alec's hand out of Kennard's. "Ignore him. He's an insatiable flirt," he said, smiling warmly at his English friend. "But yes, Alec was very brave and clever."

"You forgot handsome and good in bed," Alec added.

Cronin blushed and Kennard clapped his hands as he laughed. "Oh, how I like you." Then Kennard gave the barman a nod, "Get my friend here whatever he wants."

Alec ordered a scotch and lime water, rather thankful he didn't have to pay, because the only money he had was American dollars.

They followed Kennard through the crowd, up a few stairs, to a booth on a platform. It was clearly Kennard's table, where he could sit and watch over his club. It also gave them privacy to speak freely without fear of being overheard by human ears. When they were seated, Kennard was still smiling at Alec. "So, the key is still human," he said. "I have to say Cronin, I'm surprised."

"Yeah well, about that," Alec said, sipping his drink. "I can't be changed. Not for the lack of trying." He craned his neck slightly so his jacket slid down his neck, knowing Kennard would see the bite marks.

Kennard's eyes shot to Cronin's, and he sucked back a breath. "What is the meaning of this?"

"We don't know," Cronin said, his arm sliding protectively around Alec's shoulders. "His blood is... special. It's what made him the key to defeating Keket in Egypt—he resurrected a mummified vampire with his blood alone," Cronin said. "Though our seer says his work is not yet done."

Kennard's eyes narrowed, but he shook it off and schooled his features with a smile. He looked again at Alec's neck. "Well, if any one of us were fortunate enough to have the best of both worlds, Cronin, it would be you."

Alec finished his drink, Kennard waved his hand, and not a moment later another full drink was on the table. "Thank you," Alec said. "And thank you for helping us in Egypt. I'm glad I got to thank you in person."

"It is I who should be thanking you," Kennard said. "It's not every day we get to meet and talk with a key."

Alec was beginning to hate that word.

Maybe he wouldn't hate it so much if he knew what it fucking meant.

Kennard was still obviously shocked. "Yet you can bite him and he remains human?"

Alec swore he heard a rush of whispers from the edges of the crowd. The vampires in the club clearly heard what Kennard said. Cronin let out a low growl. Kennard raised a hand dismissively and the whispers stopped. Cronin's growl lowered but took a while to fade completely.

Kennard laughed. "Maybe we shouldn't talk about biting here, no?"

Cronin's reply was low and final. "No."

Kennard changed the subject of conversation. "How's Eiji? Is he getting better?"

"All but healed," Cronin answered. Word had spread quickly that Eiji had survived exposure to sunlight in saving Alec's life. "He and Jodis are in Japan while he convalesces."

Alec finished his drink, and a third appeared in front of him. He was already a little buzzed, so he sipped his next drink and scanned the floor while Cronin and Kennard talked of vampire matters. It was all rather political, and

Alec was too busy checking out the dance floor to pay any attention. He wasn't one to dance often, but in the end, it got the better of him. Alec downed his drink and stood up. "I'm gonna hit the dance floor," he said.

Cronin started to object, naturally, but Kennard put his hand on Cronin's arm. "Ah, Cronin," Alec heard Kennard say. "Let him dance while we talk business. No need for the three of us to be bored senseless."

Not caring they had company, Alec leaned down and kissed Cronin soundly before going back down the stairs and making his way through a sea of people. They were a mix of men and women, and from the lingering, *knowing* looks by some of them, Alec knew they were a solid mix of human and vampire.

Alec didn't care. He let his head fall back and closed his eyes, feeling the bass of the music in his chest. It felt good to be doing something so normal, so human. He knew Cronin never took his eyes off him, and once upon a time that would've annoyed Alec. He'd have forbidden such possessive behavior, but now he reveled in it. He craved being owned by Cronin, as much as Cronin longed to be owned by him.

Being fated was a beautiful thing.

Alec couldn't believe he'd once tried to rebuke the idea.

A warm body pressed a little too close, making Alec open his eyes. He knew it had to be some human—no vampire in the club would be stupid enough to approach another vampire's mate, and Cronin's mate no less. It was a guy who smiled at him, but before he could even speak, Cronin was in between them, staring at the now-pale human man until he backed away.

Alec pulled himself against Cronin's ass and laughed. "Jealousy looks good on you."

"We must leave," Cronin said.

"He didn't mean anything by it," Alec started to say.

But Cronin had Alec's hand and was leading him to what Alec realized was the back way to the fire escape. "No, we must go. Now."

Alec knew from Cronin's tone something was wrong. He tried to clear his head. "What happened?"

"It's not what *has* happened," Cronin said as he pushed through the back door into an alley where Kennard stood waiting. "It's what's *going to* happen."

Alec had no sooner stepped into the alley, than Cronin looked around and checked that the three of them were alone. He put his arm around Alec, pulled him close, put his hand on Kennard's shoulder, and they leapt.

CHAPTER TWO

AS SOON AS they'd landed wherever Cronin had leapt them to, Alec took in his surroundings. He was never sure what would greet them, if they would arrive in a vampire-filled warehouse for a coven meeting or a deserted battle-field in Scotland. So his senses were always alert, and he took in every detail.

It was night, of course. They were outside, surrounded by trees. The air was humid and thick, and smelled of cloying undergrowth and rain. No, not rain. Rain*forest*. The trees towered over them, the ground was damp underfoot, and the warning cries of exotic animals told Alec he was far from home.

"Where are we?"

Cronin kept him close. "We are in the forests near Rurrenabaque, Northern Bolivia."

"I'm gonna assume you mean the Bolivia in South America?" Alec said, trying to see past the closest tree, then into the darkened canopy. "And not the Bolivia in North Carolina, right?"

Kennard snorted quietly. "Correct."

"There is a vampire here we need to speak to," Cronin said. He nodded at the darkness ahead. "He lives just through there." He started walking, slowly, no doubt to allow for the human who couldn't see too well in the dark. "Though there is something you should know before we meet him."

Alec almost tripped over a tree root. "Oh yeah? And what's that?"

"He's a child," Cronin said.

"A vampire child?" Alec repeated. "Is that even legal?"

Kennard snorted again. "It's not preferred, no. They pose a risk to our secrecy, but this one is... different."

Cronin helped Alec navigate his footing in the dark and said, "His name is Jorge. It is believed his human parents disowned him as a small child, around a hundred years ago. Villagers were superstitious about such things and cast him out so as not to anger the gods."

"What was wrong with him?" Alec asked. His eyes had adjusted to the dark now, just in time for them to stop walking.

"We believe, in his human form, he suffered from dissociative identity disorder because, well—" Cronin made a face. "—he has taken that form in his vampiric life. He talks to himself as though he is two people. One is pleasant, one is... not."

Alec wasn't even surprised. After Egypt, nothing surprised him when it came to vampires. "Like Dr. Jekyll and Mr. Hyde?"

Cronin nodded. "Yes."

"In the one vampire?"

"Yes."

"Oh, great."

"Adelmo is his caregiver," Cronin continued to explain.

"He's a kind vampire who taught Jorge our laws. Jorge needs constant care, as he is and will always be, just a child."

Alec considered this. "Excuse my curiosity and my insolence for asking, but if he posed such a threat to vampires, why not just kill him?"

"He has a certain skill set," Kennard said. "A valuable one. His caregiver or owner, if you will, uses the boy for his own purposes."

Alec couldn't believe what he was hearing. "He what?"

"He does not harm the child," Cronin said, knowing what Alec was thinking. "In fact, quite the opposite. He treats the child as if he were his own. Adelmo cares for the boy, and the boy can warn him if there is danger."

"What's the skill set?" Alec pressed. "What can this boy do?"

"He is a seer, a very good one," Cronin answered.

"He tells the future," Kennard furthered. "He sees everything. Unlike other seers like your Eleanor, who gets snippets and flashes, nothing is hidden from Jorge."

Alec knew there was something they weren't telling him. "What's the drawback? I mean there has to be a drawback, or he wouldn't be hidden away living out here in the middle of a forest."

Cronin smiled ruefully. "He speaks in riddles."

"His visions are accurate, like no other," Kennard said. "You just need to decipher what they mean."

Cronin nodded. "And the dual conversations are a little unnerving."

"How Adelmo lives with it, I'll never know," Kennard added.

"He loves the child," Cronin said simply.

In silence, they started walking again, and after a few

hundred yards, they stopped at a clearing. It took Alec a second to notice the hut at the back of the clearing. There were no lights on inside, then Alec realized, of course, there wouldn't be. Vampires didn't need them.

Despite the hut being a good eighty yards away, Cronin spoke with a normal voice. "Adelmo, it is Cronin. I bring with me Kennard and Alec. We need to speak with Jorge."

"You bring a human," a voice replied, Alec strained to hear it. "I can hear its heart beating from here."

"The human is with me," Cronin stated flatly. "He is not to be harmed."

Alec wanted to say, "The *human* has a fucking name," but figured it might not be the icebreaker he should aim for.

Alec still didn't even know what they were doing here or what it was this kid vampire could see. But he trusted Cronin completely and knew he'd find out answers soon enough.

"You may come in," the voice said. It was stilted English with a strong Spanish accent, and Alec realized Cronin— who spoke many languages—had started the conversation in English for Alec's benefit. They walked to the hut and the door opened, though it was too dark for Alec to see inside.

Cronin stepped through the doorway first, and a moment later, he held an old lantern that diffused a soft light over the hut. He smiled at Alec, seemingly pleased with himself to have thought of Alec's needs. Alec stepped inside and was shocked by what he saw.

The hut was humble, filled with simple furniture. A man, who Alec assumed was Adelmo, stood by the table. He was tall and thin, with kind eyes, a broad forehead, and thick black hair braided down his back. He appeared to be no more than thirty in human years. Despite Adelmo's threadbare, somewhat-modern clothes, he reminded Alec of the images he'd seen of Inca warriors, and Alec wondered just how old Adelmo was. Regardless, Alec liked him immediately, but what shocked Alec was the child sitting at the table.

Jorge was possibly the cutest kid Alec had ever seen. He could be no more than six years old, with shaggy black hair, bright eyes, and rosy chubby cheeks. He was clearly excited to have company, and Alec wondered how a cute-looking kid could be so... what did Cronin call it? *Unnerving?*

Then Jorge smiled, and Alec had to stop himself from taking a step backwards.

Jorge's mouth was full of small, squared baby teeth, and vampire fangs. He laughed and said something in what Alec assumed to be a local dialect of Spanish. Alec knew some Spanish, and could make out the words *human* and *pet*, and he laughed. Then Jorge asked Adelmo, in English, "Can we have one?"

Alec could feel Cronin tense beside him as he spoke back to them in short, angry clips of their dialect of Spanish. Alec didn't need to understand every word to know Cronin didn't like what Jorge had said.

Adelmo put his hand on Jorge's shoulder, quick to pacify. "He means no harm."

"I know," Alec said. And truthfully, Alec understood. Kids had a tact all their own and weren't inhibited by social etiquette. Alec looked at Jorge. "My name is Alec. Nice to meet you."

Jorge smiled that innocent/evil smile. "We are Jorge." Then he looked at Cronin and Kennard and addressed them both by name. "Jorge we are. How can he know that? Of course he knows that." Then he seemed to argue with himself for a moment.

Okay, so the kid referred to himself in third person and

as though there were more than one of him. Alec's *disturbing meter* pinged. And sure, the kid looked five or six, but Alec had to remind himself that he was closer to a hundred years old.

Everything about him was contradictory.

But he obviously knew Cronin and Kennard and spoke to them like he'd seen them both just last week. "Hello. Jorge happy to see you again."

"We come seeking news," Cronin started to say. "I am not sure if you heard of the trouble in Egypt some months ago."

"We saw it, saw it we did," Jorge said. "Sand and dust. Such poor old souls."

"Yes," Cronin said, his tone neutral.

Then Jorge looked straight at Alec. "This one killed them all. From his blood comes the sun," he said. Then he snarled. "They knew not what they did."

Cronin clearly didn't appreciate the child's tone, but Alec put his hand on Cronin's arm and stopped him from speaking. Alec looked straight at the small boy. "He's right. Jorge is right. The sun came from my blood, and yes, it killed them all. Those returned vampires didn't know what they were doing. The woman who made them was very cruel. She refused to feed them and teach them. They didn't know what they were doing was wrong."

"They were a clear threat to our kind," Cronin said.

Adelmo nodded and bowed, almost apologetically. "He knows this."

All the while, Jorge mumbled and argued with himself, going from angry to sweet in the blink of an eye. "So wrong. No it wasn't. Tell our secrets, they would have. How? No teachings of rules. Jorge hates rules." Then when he was done in English, he started again in Spanish.

If Alec had wondered why Jorge hadn't been 'acquired' by larger, more powerful covens, he now knew why.

Jorge was forever a child, with the attention span and temper to match. And that was without the creepy double personalities that talked to each other in fluent conversation. Both personalities seemed present at the same time, and like most kids who didn't like sharing toys, Jorge seemed to be in a constant state of flux, one personality always bickering with the other. He reminded Alec, very sadly, of Sméagol from *The Lord of the Rings*.

After he was done arguing with himself, Jorge laughed again and smiled delightedly at Alec. Whether it was because Alec had agreed with him, or if he just found it amusing that a human would speak to him at all, or if the kid was just pure batshit crazy, Alec didn't know. He looked from Cronin to Alec and back again, and his smile was now an angry glare. "It wasn't the Queen who did wrong." He glowered for a long moment. "Jorge not happy. No, not happy."

Kennard, obviously trying to steer the conversation forward, looked at the boy and said, "We were wondering if Jorge has seen anything else that might jeopardize the secrecy of our kind."

Then Cronin added, "Specifically in China, or even Russia."

Alec looked quizzically at Cronin, something Jorge didn't miss. The small boy gave Alec a fanged and toothy smile that was more menacing than jovial.

Kennard said, "I heard a vampire coven from southern Russia had gone north, asking for clemency for invading territories. And that is something that doesn't sit well with me."

Cronin followed with, "Coincidentally, just today I

read of a string of unexplained disappearances in and around Shaanxi Province, China. Their police is investigating a suspect serial killer."

"And you believe them to be related?" Adelmo asked.

"I'd rather not take the risk. Given such rumors were how the mess in Egypt started," Cronin said simply.

All the while, Jorge hadn't taken his eyes off Alec. He looked at him with a childish wonder, and Alec couldn't help himself. He slowly pulled a chair out from the table and sat down next to Jorge.

Now, Alec didn't have a great deal of experience with kids, but he knew enough that sitting down with them and meeting them at eye level was a good way to start. "Cronin tells me you've got quite a talent," Alec said.

The boy smiled. "We can see *dos*." He held up two fingers.

"Two?" Alec didn't really know what that meant, but he went along with it.

Jorge nodded. "Eyes and mind. Eyes and mind, here and gone, Jorge sees." Then he frowned. "Of course he understands."

Okay, he could see with his eyes and his mind. Alec nodded. "That's pretty cool."

"Jorge doesn't like it," Jorge said. "Not everything he sees is good. No, not everything he sees is good."

"Must be a bit scary sometimes," Alec agreed. He couldn't imagine seeing the horrors he saw in Egypt in graphic mental images as a six-year-old kid.

"You not afraid of Jorge," Jorge said. "He should be afraid. Humans are always afraid. Not this one."

Alec smiled and nodded pointedly at Cronin. "I'm not afraid at all."

"Cronin es el marido de Alec," Jorge said. "Yes, *marido marido.* Jorge sees it."

Alec wracked his memory for Spanish. *Marido, marido....* "Husband? Is Cronin my husband?" Alec snorted. Well, for all intents and purposes, especially to a six year old kid, he guessed he was. Alec smiled at Cronin. "Yes, he is. Sort of."

"Fuerte destino," Jorge said. "Jorge sees fuerte destino. Strong fate, in English so the human comprenda." He was frowning now, as though one personality was arguing and scowling at the other. "Red hand in the stones. Yes, yes."

Okay, he lost Alec on most of that, except for the fate part. "Yes, fate," Alec said. Wanting to distract Jorge a little, he looked around the room and noticed a soccer ball in the corner. Alec nodded toward it. "You like to play?"

Then Jorge snarled, his eyes full of rage. "Jorge cannot play. No, not allowed to play."

Oh, shit. Okay then. Thankfully Adelmo clarified. "He cannot play with the village children."

"Oh, right," Alec said, nodding slowly. That must suck as a perpetual child, to never have any friends. *So, why the hell not.* "I could play with you?" he asked. Alec was pretty sure Cronin was about to object or pop a vessel in his forehead, but Alec wouldn't be deterred. He smiled at Jorge. "Though I bet you'd be too good for me."

Jorge obviously liked this development. Before Alec could blink, Jorge got up, retrieved the ball, and stood in front of Alec. His eyes were dark, his cheeks still a rosy red, and his little fangs dominated his smile. And he handed the ball to Alec.

Now, Alec had never played American football. His father, being Scottish, had objected to anything that wasn't traditional football, or soccer as the other kids had called it. But he also hadn't picked up a soccer ball in over a decade. He stood up in the small hut, and knowing all eyes were on him and hoping like all hell he didn't make an ass of himself, he dropped the ball, catching it with his foot. He balanced the ball on one foot, then kicked it to his other and back again.

Jorge laughed and clapped his hands. "Jorge do it, Jorge do it."

Of course with his vampire agility and reflexes, he did the footwork with masterful skill.

"See? You're too good for me!" Alec said, snatching back the ball. He quickly spun it on his fingertip like basketball players do.

Jorge laughed and bounced on his toes. "Jorge do it, Jorge do it." He snatched the ball back and again performed the trick like he'd done it all his life.

Still smiling, Alec sat back down at the table and glanced at Cronin. He seemed concerned and confused but, of course, said nothing. Then Jorge took Alec's hand, startling Alec a little, and studied his watch.

"You like it?" Alec said.

"Jorge will have it," the small vampire child said. "Yes, Jorge will have it."

Adelmo intervened. "No, Jorge, it's not yours. It belongs to Alec."

The boy glowered and bared his fangs, snarling a little. Alec now understood why Jorge needed a parental caregiver. He was certain, if left unsupervised, Jorge and his childish temper could level a small village if he got angry enough. It was clear Adelmo spent a great deal of time reminding Jorge of his manners.

Alec smiled at Jorge. "You know what? You can have it," he said, undoing his watch. It wasn't anything expensive, and it wasn't like Alec needed to be on time to go anywhere. He handed the wristwatch to Jorge, and the little boy looked up at him and smiled, fangs and all, when he took the watch.

Jorge sat on the chair next to Alec again, his feet not touching the floor, and clasped the too-big watch on his own wrist. "The time of the key," Jorge mumbled to himself. "Jorge has the time of the key."

Alec glanced at Cronin, then back to Jorge. "That's right. The time of the key."

When Jorge looked up, his eyes were closed but they twitched with REM, as though he was looking into the depths of his own mind. "From his blood comes the sun," Jorge said again. "Blood from a stone. Stone from a blood." Jorge was quiet for a moment, his eyes still closed but moving. "So many questions. Blood from a stone."

When Jorge looked up, his eyes were black. Alec's blood ran cold.

Jorge's voice was different, and he spoke in perfect English, like he'd been possessed. "Red hand, blue moon, silver river, the earth will come to life. Blood from a stone, stone from a blood. He is risen already, as she was risen, the answer is in the stones. Blood from a stone, stone from a blood."

Cronin spoke next. "What does the key need to do?"

"Blue moon, silver river, blood from a stone. You will not find him with your eyes." He looked at Alec like he was seeing straight through him. "Yes, through the key. Through the key."

Then Jorge shook his head a little and his eyes returned to normal. He grinned his little fanged smile, like he hadn't just impersonated the kid from *The Omen*. "Jorge will see you again," he said cheerfully.

Alec wasn't sure if it was a vision or a request. He nodded nonetheless. "Sure."

Cronin put a hand on Alec's shoulder. "Thank you, Jorge, Adelmo," he said with a nod. "It is most appreciated."

"I hope you got what you came for," Adelmo said. Alec didn't know whether Adelmo was used to the random ramblings of Jorge, if he was used to the black eyes, or if he didn't care about what he'd just seen. He made no attempt to translate.

Cronin gave a nod, as did Kennard. They spoke at the same time. "Thank you."

Cronin held his hand out to Alec, which he took as his cue to leave. He grabbed it quickly, but before he left, he held out his spare hand toward Jorge. "High five."

Little Jorge's face lit up and he jumped up quickly to slap Alec's hand, and they walked out the door, leaving the vampire child giggling behind them.

"Red hands in the stones. Forever is in the stones," Jorge said. Alec, Cronin, and Kennard turned to face the little boy. He grinned his cute and creepy grin. "The key asks different questions, he does. Yes, he does. Red hands in the stones. Forever is in the stones."

Alec had no clue what that was supposed to mean, but he gave the kid a smile and a nod. Cronin ushered Alec along, and four steps into the clearing, Cronin—still holding Alec's hand—reached out and touched Kennard's arm, and they were gone.

THEY WERE BACK in the London alley, behind Kennard's nightclub. Alec shivered from the abrupt change of temperature, from humid heat to freezing cold, and Cronin pulled him close, rubbing his back for warmth.

Alec had never been so glad to be somewhere else. He looked up the wet, darkened alley. "Oh, thank God. Back in the land of the normal."

Kennard laughed. His voice sounded very British after hearing so much Spanish. "He sure is different."

Alec shivered, this time not from the abrupt change in temperature. Out of all the vampires Alec had seen, including the rabid batshit-fucking crazy Egyptian Goddess vampire Keket, Jorge was by far the most frightening. "So innocent and so disturbingly evil."

Cronin rubbed his back. "It's an unnerving combination, yes?"

Kennard laughed. "Well, he liked you."

"I just figured it was best to make friends with him," Alec said. "Get him on our side, ya know? At first, I didn't think he was gonna tell us anything, so I figured I'd talk to him on his level."

"Well, it worked," Kennard said. "What did you make of that whole blood in the stone, red hand thing?"

"I don't know yet," Cronin answered. "It's a puzzle we need to put together."

Kennard clearly thought so too. "I'm sure as more comes to light, as more covens move, or rumors are spread, we can piece it together."

Cronin nodded. "Agreed."

"You guys knew something was going on?" Alec asked. "In China or Russia or some-freakin'-where."

"Only what I read in the newspaper of repeated disappearances," Cronin explained. "Then tonight, Kennard said he'd heard of covens relocating."

"And that's a red flag?"

Cronin nodded. "I should have told you."

"Yes, you should have," Alec said.

Kennard clapped Alec on the arm. "I'm sure if we need to know anything more, we can ask him again. Jorge has a friend in you."

Alec could only shake his head. "Man, I know he's just a kid and all, but the mood swings are off the charts. Adelmo should consider cutting back that kid's preservatives. Go let him feed on some vegans or something."

Cronin snorted and Kennard burst out laughing. "Oh Alec, you are a charm."

Cronin held Alec a little too close, and the gruffness in Cronin's voice was one he knew well. "We should be returning home."

Alec, fitting so perfectly against Cronin, agreed. Unable to help himself, he ran his hand down over the swell of Cronin's ass and ran his nose along his neck. "Yes, it's been hours."

"Yes," Kennard said with a laugh. "I forgot what it was like to be around newly fated couples." He shook his whole body. "Now I need to go find someone to enjoy the pheromones with, thanks."

Alec laughed. "You're welcome." He slid both arms around Cronin and scraped his teeth against Cronin's jaw and the next thing he knew, he was on his back in the middle of Cronin's bed. His shirt was gone, his legs were spread, and Cronin knelt between them. He smiled around his fangs, his eyes a salacious black.

Alec moaned and raised his hips. He closed his eyes and exposed his neck and waited for the pleasure to take him.

CHAPTER THREE

ALEC HIT STOP on the treadmill, slowing to a walk. "Did you talk to them?"

Cronin had been on the phone to Eiji. He nodded. "Yes. They'll be back in an hour. So when you're ready, we can go."

Alec wiped his face down and stepped off the treadmill. "I'll just go shower. You know, it'll be twice as quick if you helped me."

Cronin laughed. "It'll be twice as long. I know what your intentions are."

Alec grinned as he walked past him. He flicked the towel at Cronin's ass, hitting him with a smart thwack. Alec took off and Cronin chased him, which ended with the two of them laughing through soapy hand jobs in the shower, which lead to more fooling around in bed, which of course ended with them being late to meet Eiji and Jodis.

They were still all hands and smiles when they leapt into the small living room of the Tokyo house. It was one of Cronin's houses—he had three: a house in Japan, an apartment in London, and the apartment in New York City that

Alec now called home, though Alec always assumed the Japanese home was more for Eiji than Cronin. Alec had been to the Tokyo house once before, when Cronin leapt them all here so Eiji could heal in peace.

He'd suffered exposure to sunlight in their battle against Queen Keket in Egypt and had almost died. It was Alec's blood that had saved him, a source of rich sustenance at just the right time, or so Alec believed.

It had been almost eight weeks ago that Eiji and Jodis came to Japan, and although Cronin hadn't said as much, Alec knew he missed his friends.

When Alec had asked, Cronin said they hadn't spent a whole eight weeks apart in a long time. He guessed a vampire's version of "a long time" was a few hundred years, so that would explain Cronin's excitement to see them.

When Alec and Cronin finally pulled away from each other, they found Jodis and Eiji standing by the rice paper wall, smiling at them.

"Look at you," Jodis said, looking at Cronin. "I've never seen you smile so."

Cronin walked over to his oldest friend and pulled her in for a quick embrace. "Jodis, my dear, how are you?"

"Fine, fine," she said with a warm smile.

Alec was quick to hug Eiji. "Eiji, my man, how are you?"

The smaller Japanese vampire laughed. "Better. Much better," he said.

When Alec let go of him, he realized he'd missed Eiji's smiling face. "Well, you look great."

"And look at you two," Eiji said. "I assume the last weeks have been well-spent."

Cronin blushed and Alec laughed. "Something like that."

"Well, it warms my heart to see it," Jodis said. She tilted her head. "Though we grew worried when you were late in arriving."

"Oh, well," Cronin said, fighting a smile. "That was Alec's fault."

Alec barked out a laugh. "Really? Because I seem to recall you—"

Jodis put up her hand to stop Alec mid-sentence. "Uh. No need for details."

"Come and sit down," Eiji said, waving his hand at the sofas. "Tell us Cronin, you said you spoke to Jorge? What on Earth for?"

They sat down and Cronin quickly took Alec's hand. "I read of reported disappearances in Northern China. I didn't think much of it, but we went to London and met with Kennard and he mentioned in passing about word of a Russian coven fleeing their territory."

Eiji and Jodis were both silent and still, their faces serious. Alec was learning that this red flag of vampire behavior —of covens fleeing their own territories—was never a good thing.

"So we left London and went directly to Bolivia to see Jorge," Cronin continued. He smiled at Alec. "He liked Alec."

"The kid was a weird one, that's for sure," Alec said, making Eiji laugh. "But I mean, it's not his fault. He can't help what he is. No vampire chooses their talent, right?"

"Or their mental well-being," Jodis said. "Jorge is quite unique in that regard. He's the only one in all our kind to have dual personalities."

"Thank God," Alec said. He looked at the three vampires. "He's probably the scariest vampire I've encountered."

Eiji snorted incredulously. "He's not even four feet tall."

Alec shivered. "He gave me the heebie-jeebies. You know when the hairs on the back of your neck stand on end?"

Cronin raised an eyebrow at Alec. "Do you always play football with people who scare you?"

Jodis' eyes went wide. "You played football with him?"

"Not really," Alec answered nonchalantly. "Just some ball skills. I didn't think he was going to tell us anything."

"And what did he tell you?" Eiji asked.

"He was cryptic, as usual," Cronin replied. "He said 'Red hand, blue moon, silver river, the earth will come to life. Blood from a stone, stone from a blood. He is risen already, as she was risen, the answer is in the stones. Blood from a stone, stone from a blood.'"

Alec added, "Then Cronin asked him what the key had to do, and he said 'Blue moon, silver river, blood from a stone. You will not find him with your eyes. Through the key. Through the key.'" Alec raised both eyebrows. "The kid needs meds or something."

Cronin laughed proudly. "Alec suggested the child feed only from vegans to reduce preservatives in his diet."

Eiji laughed again, his whole face smiling. "Oh Alec, I have missed you."

Jodis turned serious. "What does it all mean?"

Cronin took a deep breath and squeezed Alec's hand. "I think Alec's duty as the key, whatever it is, has started again."

Eiji shook his head at Alec. "We just can't keep you out of trouble, can we?"

"I try," Alec said with a shrug, "but it just keeps finding me."

"Cronin," Jodis whispered. "Blue moon? There will be a blue moon this month."

Cronin was stoic, his answer quiet. "I know."

"What does that mean?" Alec asked. "A blue moon is the second full moon in any given month, right?"

"Yes," Eiji answered. "Though typically it meant a fourth full moon in any season, but yes, close enough."

"So when's the next full moon?"

"Next week," Cronin said, giving him a tight smile. "At least we have a time frame now."

"We need to go back to New York," Jodis said. "We're better equipped there."

Alec looked around the small Japanese house. He loved the white rice paper walls, dark timber trims, the low-set furniture, the bare essentials. It was out of the city, far removed from the road for passersby to notice. Granted Alec had only ever seen it at night, but he felt at peace there. He always seemed to be racing against time, and he wanted to savor one night of some fun before the serious work began. "What time is it here?" Alec asked.

"Ten-thirty at night," Cronin said. "Why?"

He shrugged. "Well, yes, we probably should head back to New York at some point." He smiled. "But I've never been to Tokyo."

Cronin squeezed his hand. "Then I shall take you." He looked over at Eiji. "Are you up for a tour?"

"Yes, of course," Eiji said. "I really do feel much better." He grinned at Alec. "You'll love it."

"Different much since you were a boy?"

Eiji laughed again. Alec really had missed the sound. "In ways you cannot imagine."

Alec jumped to his feet and pulled Cronin up. "Well,

considering the key, meaning me, is on another time crunch, I say we don't waste a minute."

When Cronin was ready to leap the four of them somewhere in downtown Tokyo, Alec put his hand on Eiji's arm and a look of disbelief crossed Cronin's face. He leapt before Alec could ask him what was wrong.

THE NEXT THING ALEC KNEW, he was in a dark secluded alley, but the sounds of a bustling city were everywhere. He looked up the short alley and saw streams of people walking past, and when they got to the junction of where the alley met the street, Alec was speechless.

Sure, he'd seen pictures and movies of Tokyo, but nothing, *nothing* prepared him for what it was like in real life.

If Times Square was lit up like a lantern, then Shibuya Station was a freakin' Christmas tree.

Shops, restaurants, people—so many people—and the neon lit advertising signs made it look like daytime.

"Wow," Alec said.

Cronin took his hand. Alec didn't even have to look at him to know he was smiling. It was in his voice. "It's remarkable, isn't it?"

"Come on," he said, pulling him into the flow of pedestrians. If something was wrong before, it seemed forgotten. Cronin pointed things out in window fronts, while Eiji and Jodis walked arm in arm behind them. Alec felt oddly like he was a kid being chaperoned, but they were lost in their own conversation.

"It's good to see them again," Alec said quietly. They'd stopped at a window front, and Eiji and Jodis were half a block back by then. If they heard Alec, they never let on.

"It is," Cronin agreed, smiling as he looked at the displays.

"You missed them," Alec stated. "I did too. They kind of grow on you."

Cronin laughed. "Have I not kept you busy enough that you long for the company of others?"

Alec snorted and nudged Cronin with his elbow. "You know what I mean."

"Do you like that one?" Cronin asked, pointing to a black and silver watch in the display.

Alec balked. "Um, yeah. But I'm pretty sure I wouldn't like the price tag." He glanced up at the exclusive brand name above his head.

Cronin scoffed. "Alec, it's not as though it's a Patek Philippe."

Alec's mouth fell open. He knew those watches sold for well over a million. "Uh. No." He shook his head. "Don't even think about it." Alec could barely contemplate it.

Cronin laughed and led him inside the store. He greeted the woman behind the counter in fluent Japanese, surprising Alec more than her. And in two minutes, Cronin had picked out the watch, made the woman giggle three times, and paid for his purchase. Alec saw all the zeros on the credit card screen, and his voice squeaked. "Please tell me that's in yen."

Cronin laughed, but he took the watch and put it on Alec's wrist. Alec knew Cronin had money and real estate and cash and whatever, and Alec had tried to not let the fact bother him that he came into Cronin's apartment with a frozen bank account and nothing more than clothes and an old laptop. But when he saw the pride, the satisfaction, and the joy on Cronin's face when he put the watch on his wrist, he couldn't bring himself to argue.

It took his breath away.

So instead of whining about unnecessary extravagance or refusing the gift completely, he was so humbled by the love on Cronin's face, all he could do was offer a choked out, "Thank you."

Cronin smiled, the eye-crinkling kind of smile, before thanking the saleswoman again, taking Alec's hand, and walking outside to where Eiji and Jodis were waiting. Alec was certain Eiji smiled all day long, but Jodis' happiness was aimed directly at Cronin and how content he was. It clearly pleased her, very much. And Alec adored her for it.

He showed them the watch. "And I promise not to give this one to Jorge."

Alec expected a laugh or a roll of the eyes or something, but all three vampires turned their heads in perfect sync to something humans obviously could not hear.

Eiji and Jodis turned back around, but Cronin's head remained turned. When he looked back, his face was ashen, his dark eyes were wild, and he looked... afraid?

"Cronin," Alec whispered. "What is it?"

He shook his head. "We need to leave. Now."

No one argued. And for one long beat, Alec thought Cronin might leap them in full public view. He paused, then all but dragged Alec by the hand into the nearest darkened side street. Eiji and Jodis followed like Cronin's shadow, then he spun on his heel and the four of them disappeared.

CRONIN'S NEW YORK CITY apartment was brightly lit, making Alec blink back the glare, and their feet had no sooner hit the ground before Jodis and Eiji swarmed around protectively.

"Cronin!" they said in unison.

"What is it?" Jodis asked.

"Tell us, brother, what is wrong?" Eiji pleaded. He wasn't smiling now.

Cronin kept a tight hold on Alec, seemingly reluctant to let him go. "Something's wrong," Cronin said meekly. He swallowed hard and looked at Alec with apology in his eyes. "With me."

CHAPTER FOUR

ALEC'S first reaction was to laugh. Because seriously, Cronin was the most perfect specimen of man or vampire he'd ever met. How could anything be wrong with him?

But Eiji and Jodis weren't laughing. In fact, they looked deeply concerned, and Cronin's expression matched theirs. And it was that look, that not-confident, not-assured, and un-knowing look on his face that spread a dull and heavy dread through Alec's body.

"Tell us," Jodis said quickly.

Cronin's swallowed again. "I noticed it in England first. At the bar. There were several vampires there, most of them I recognized. Lars was there," he said.

"You called him by name, in the bar," Alec interrupted. "I wondered who he was."

"He's a vampire with the talent of pyrokinesis."

Alec blanched. "He can start *fires* with his *mind?*"

Cronin nodded. "He was standing at the bar, and when he looked at me, I swear I felt warmth"—he held out his hand—"in my fingers."

Jodis and Eiji both blinked, shocked.

Cronin kept talking. "Then in Bolivia with Jorge. We stood in his house, and he started to see his visions and"—he looked at Jodis—"I saw flashes of light in my mind. No images or anything with form, just flashes."

Alec had noticed Cronin look a little stunned in that hut, though he'd just presumed it was from what Jorge was saying.

Then he looked at Eiji. "When we leapt to Tokyo, I touched your hand. What I saw was...." He shook his head. "I think I saw what you see. A timeline of dots and patterns, how scientists read DNA. Just for the briefest moment."

Now Eiji's face was blank with shock. He nodded.

"And just now on the street in Tokyo," Cronin said. "We all smelled that vampire."

Jodis nodded woodenly. "Yes," she whispered.

"Well, I heard him," Cronin said. "In my mind. I heard his thoughts."

Eiji was stunned, and after a long few seconds, he shook his head. "I don't understand."

"Neither do I," Cronin replied, his voice just a whisper. "It is as though I get glimpses of their talents. I can't begin to explain it."

Jodis eyed him cautiously. "And what of my talent," she said. "If I concentrate."

Cronin hissed, though it was Alec who pulled away. "Ow." The three vampires looked at him questioningly as he rubbed the hand Cronin had been holding. "Uh, freezer burn."

A horrified looking Cronin put both his hands up. "*Nas duilghe na ghabhas cur ann an cainnt*," Cronin whispered, shaking his head. His eyes were a sorry black. Alec knew when Cronin spoke Gaelic, his native Scottish tongue, it was straight from the heart. "I am more sorry than words can say. Alec, please."

Alec didn't hesitate. He threw his arms around Cronin and pulled him tight against him. "Hey. Don't apologize. It didn't hurt."

When Alec looked over Cronin's head to Jodis and Eiji, they both looked catatonic with shock. "We will find out what this is," Alec said. "Yes?"

Jodis blinked, then blinked again, her blue eyes imploring. "When was the last time you fed?"

Cronin pulled away from Alec and answered weakly. "I've um, I've been feeding from Alec."

Well, if they weren't shocked before, they were now. "You haven't fed from another source?" Eiji asked.

Cronin shook his head. "I've not left Alec alone, and well...." He smiled sadly and blushed. "We've um...."

"We've been having a lot of sex," Alec finished for him, not embarrassed at all. "And he bites me every time. I like it. Actually, I love it. And he's been having a lot of small amounts. He hasn't been hungry at all."

Jodis and Eiji both looked between Alec and Cronin for a full ten seconds. "I don't know what to make of this," Jodis said, shaking her head slowly. "Alec's blood is powerful, yes? That's what Eleanor said. She said there was something special about your blood, didn't she?"

Alec nodded. "You think it's my blood that's doing this to him?"

"What else could it be?" she replied. "Cronin, you seem to be acquiring the talent of a transfer."

Alec knew what that was. Cronin once told him that a transfer was a vampire who could mimic the power of another vampire if he were close enough. They simply transferred the talent into themselves. The host never lost their ability, the transfer simply acquired it.

Cronin shook his head slowly. "How is that even possible?"

Both Jodis and Eiji shook their heads. "I don't know," they said in unison.

Jodis put her hand on Cronin's arm. "Cronin, I think you should go feed. Maybe it will flush your system. I don't know. Eiji will go with you. I will stay here with Alec."

Cronin looked a little unsure but he nodded, and with a simple touch on Eiji's arm, they were gone. Alec was left staring at Jodis. "What the hell does this mean?"

Now that Cronin was gone, Jodis let her worries be known. "I don't know, Alec. In all my years, I've never heard of such a thing. I don't even know if there's ever been a case of a vampire feeding from the same human more than once."

"Because they either die or turn into a vampire, right?" Alec asked.

"Exactly," she answered.

"Um, this is probably going to sound a little naïve," Alec started, "but is it necessarily a bad thing? I'd have thought getting a new talent would be a good thing?"

Jodis shook her head quickly. "We cannot change or evolve from what we are. For Cronin to experience this after twelve hundred years means something is not right."

"And it's my blood that's doing this to him?"

"It is the only thing I can see as a possible reason," she said. "Your blood is different, Alec. To what purpose, we don't yet know."

Alec was suddenly lost for words. He struggled to find the right ones. "I don't want to hurt him."

Jodis' face softened, as did her eyes. She put her hand on his arm. "I know."

Alec swallowed hard and pressed the heel of his hand against his sternum, letting out a slow breath.

"I thought the passing of weeks might have lessened the yearning," Jodis said.

"Or made it worse," Alec countered. He hadn't felt this ache in months, not since their very first times apart. He puffed out a breath. "Maybe it's because we've spent so much time together lately."

Jodis frowned. "Yes, maybe." She certainly didn't seem convinced.

Alec found that pacing, even slowly, helped with the dull weight in his chest. As did thinking of something else. "So tell me," he started. "How's Eiji been?"

Jodis watched Alec as he walked back and forth across the living room. "He's healed completely," she said. "He was in considerable pain for the first week, not that he said as much. He's more of a suffer in silence kind of man." She almost smiled. "He's a traditional Japanese man in that way; he reflects inward. And he is very sorry for almost leaving me. Not that he regrets saving you. He doesn't, but his almost dying hurt me very much, and for that he's sorry."

"I'm sorry he was hurt," Alec said. He stopped pacing. "He offered his life for me, to protect me, and I will be forever grateful."

"And you saved him with your blood, so I consider us even," she said, smiling genuinely. "There isn't a human on the planet that would have offered his blood to save a vampire."

"Except me," Alec answered. He started pacing again, taking calculated steps and deep breaths. "Although look where my blood has gotten Cronin...."

"We don't know for sure," Jodis said. "We must research what we can."

"Isn't there some vampire doctor elder we could ask?" Alec suggested. "Surely somewhere in the world, someone knows something."

"We can't ask anyone," Jodis said. "Alec, it would put Cronin at risk. If word got out that he was vulnerable, or if another coven thought him to be a risk to our kind...." She shook her head. "No, we can't ask anyone."

"What about Jorge?"

"What about him?"

"We could ask him. Everyone else on the planet thinks he's crazy anyway."

Jodis considered this. "Maybe. We'll wait to see if drinking blood that is not yours has any kind of effect on him."

Alec stopped pacing and let his hand fall from his chest. "Cronin," he whispered.

Before Jodis could question Alec, Cronin and Eiji appeared in the living room. Cronin quickly crossed the room and Alec held his arms open. The two men sighed in relief at the contact.

Despite their sudden appearance, Jodis still looked at Alec. "You knew he was returning?"

"I could feel it," Alec mumbled against the side of Cronin's head. He pulled back and looked at him. "How do you feel?"

"Better now," Cronin whispered. Alec cupped Cronin's face in his hands and pressed their lips together.

"He was anxious to return," Eiji said, looking at Jodis. "The absence of Alec was overwhelming."

"Yes," Jodis said. "Alec was no better."

"That's normal, right?" Alec asked, now with one arm around Cronin.

"Initially, yes," Jodis said. "But the longing should have waned a little, not gotten stronger."

"I wasn't too bad," Alec said.

"You were pacing like a caged lion," Jodis stated flatly.

"I'm sorry for leaving," Cronin said, looking up at Alec.

"I said I was fine," Alec said, a little softer this time, whispering it just for Cronin.

"Cronin," Jodis said quietly. "How do you feel? Did you see any of Eiji's talent when you touched him to leap just now?"

Cronin shook his head. "No. I was focusing on Alec." He looked up at Alec again. "You could feel me leaping?"

"The ache right here"—Alec put his hand to his sternum again—"started to ease."

Eiji walked up to him and held out his hand, palm up. "Tell me what you see."

Cronin held Eiji's hand and closed his eyes for a few seconds. "I see a timeline but it's not as clear. I can't define anything, but it's there."

"Okay," Jodis said, holding out her hand. "Now me."

Alec dropped his arm and stepped away. He cringed at Cronin. "Sorry, but I don't want my insides frozen."

Cronin made a face, but with a sigh, he put his hand on Jodis' arm and again, closed his eyes.

"I can feel it," Cronin said. "It's not as strong as before." He pulled his hand back and Alec quickly put his arms around him in a side-on hug. He just needed to be close to him, he needed to touch him.

"It seems to have lessened with the fresh blood," Jodis said. "We probably won't know for certain until you feed some more."

"And may I suggest not from Alec," Eiji said. He eyed them both and shook his head. "You two are quite inseparable."

"Hmm," Jodis hummed her agreement. She looked at Cronin. "Have a vampire and human ever been fated before?"

"Not that I have ever heard of," Cronin admitted.

"Me either," Eiji added.

"We have nothing to compare your situation to," Jodis said, her eyes full of worry. "Your connection is certainly strong."

Alec put his hand up. "Wait, what? Back up a minute," he said. "He can't feed from me?"

"We can't stop you," Jodis said. "Though I wouldn't recommend it. Not until we know of the long-term effects."

Eiji snorted out a laugh. "Is it that good?"

Alec let out a slow breath. "It's, um, what's the right word... heightening. There's a spot along the groin where the femoral artery runs—"

Eiji put his hand up. "Whoa, stop right there. Please."

Cronin chuckled into Alec's chest. "I don't think he wants details."

Jodis fought a smile, but as always, she was the voice of reason. "We have no way of knowing the effects on you, Cronin, nor the effects it may have on Alec. I think we need to research what we can, and maybe we should speak to Eleanor. She can be trusted with this, yes?"

"We also need to sort out Jorge's cryptic puzzle as well," Alec reminded them. He clapped Eiji on the shoulder. "Aren't you glad to be back? More mysteries to solve, more bad guys to kill. We're really just missing the Mystery Inc. van and the talking dog." The three vampires stared at Alec. He rolled his eyes. "Never mind."

Eiji snorted out a laugh. "I'm very glad to be back here," he said. "I've missed all the crazy things you say."

Alec laughed and plonked himself onto the sofa. "In the last twenty-four hours, I've been to three different countries, on three different continents, and thanks to Mr. I-only-need-two-hours-sleep-a-night here"—he nodded towards Cronin with a waggle of his eyebrows—"I didn't sleep much. I'm beat."

Cronin sat down beside him. He was instantly concerned. "Are you well?"

"I am *so* well," he replied with a smile. "I feel great actually, just tired."

Cronin took his hand. "Then you should rest. We can start researching a few things while you sleep."

Alec shook his head. "No. I think I need to use my brain. I've done nothing but use my body for the last eight weeks—"

Cronin blushed scarlet, making Eiji laugh.

"I meant with all the physical stuff I've been doing, like exercise and stuff." Alec looked pointedly at Eiji. "I've not used my brain for anything other than reading newspapers. My brain's turning to mush. Getting back into investigating work will be good for me."

"Where do you want to start?" Cronin asked.

"I think it makes sense that we research what Jorge told us," Alec said. "And Jodis and Eiji can look into vampire histories and see if there's ever been a case of this transference or a human/vampire relationship before."

"Even if there is," Jodis added, "the chances of that human being a key *and* immune to vampire bites are nil. Even if by some miracle there was, the circumstances will not be the same."

"Agreed," Cronin said with a nod. His brow creased as he frowned. "There is a library in Prague with a basement vault. They had quite the collection of vampire medical books. Maybe they still have them. I don't know, but we should start there."

"Medical?" Alec questioned.

Cronin gave him a failed smile. "Scripts that list any known talents of vampires, any issues that particular talent may have caused."

"Such as?"

"It's quite common for telepathic vampires to show signs of madness," Jodis explained. "After having so many voices in their heads for so long, they either seek out solitude or they go mad."

Alec couldn't believe it. "I thought vampires couldn't change? To become afflicted with mental illness indicates the ability to change or to be affected."

Cronin nodded slowly. "That is what I fear."

"No," Alec barked. He sat forward and took Cronin's face in his hands. "There's nothing wrong with you. You're absolutely perfect."

Cronin's dark eyes swam with doubt and vulnerability. "I have experienced talents which are not my own, Alec. Something is not right with me."

"And that is why we shan't wait," Jodis said. "Cronin, I know you are loath to leave Alec, but can you take us to this library vault you speak of now?"

Cronin nodded and stood up. He declared he would only be a minute, that Alec should stay and rest, and he put his hands on his two best friends before the three of them disappeared.

Alec sat alone in the apartment, surrounded by white

walls and silence. The familiar ache of absence exploded in his chest and he waited for Cronin to return. Though this time, absence swirled with dread. "There can't be anything wrong with you, Cronin." He swallowed the lump in his throat and spoke to the empty room. "There just can't be."

CHAPTER FIVE

PACING WASN'T HELPING ANY, so needing to distract himself, Alec grabbed a notepad and started his basic police-work routine. Starting at the beginning, he wrote down exactly what Jorge had said, and no sooner had he jotted down those few lines, than the ache in his chest and the tight hold around his heart loosened its grip. He knew Cronin would be home soon.

A moment later, Cronin, Jodis, and Eiji reappeared in the living room, and Alec almost laughed with relief. The three of them were holding books, and by the look of them, they were very old books at that.

"I hope you used your library cards for those," Alec said, standing up. He threw his notepad on the sofa and walked directly over to Cronin. "I knew you were coming back again this time. I could feel it."

Cronin tucked the books under one arm so he could kiss Alec. "And I swear I heard you talking to me."

"Really? What did I say?" Alec said with a smirk. "I hope it was dirty."

Eiji barked out a laugh. "You said there can't be

anything wrong with him. That's what he repeated to us when we were there."

Alec's smile died, and he stared at Cronin. "Tell me exactly what you heard."

Cronin's brow furrowed. "You said 'There can't be anything wrong with you, Cronin.'"

Then in complete unison, they both said, "There just can't be."

Now all three vampires stared at Alec. A shiver of fear ran down his spine. "That's what I said." He pointed to the sofa. "I sat there, thinking about how Cronin said he felt something wasn't right, and I said there can't be anything wrong with him. I said it out loud."

"Okay, this is getting more absurd," Jodis said, taking Cronin's burden of books as well as her own. "We need to start this now."

"It's not normal, is it?" Alec asked quietly. "For fated couples to hear each other."

"When they're on the other side of the world?" Eiji asked, his eyebrows raised. "Uh, no."

Alec took a deep breath and looked right into Cronin's eyes. "We need to find a doctor. One we can pay enough not to say anything."

Cronin shook his head, confused. "What for?"

"To run tests on my blood," Alec explained. "Surely they can test trace elements, abnormalities, something. Anything. If it's my blood that's doing this, and we all think it is, right?" He didn't wait for them to answer. "Then it might show something. Or it might show nothing, but at least by process of elimination we'll know more than we do right now."

Jodis smiled and gave a nod of approval. "I agree with Alec. It's a good idea."

"I know all doctors have patient confidentiality, but I can't see my family doctor. I've known him since I was a boy, and he's friends with my dad. And now that I'm technically a felon wanted by the NYPD, I can't ask him to not report me." Alec shrugged. "So how do we go about finding doctors who'll do tests but won't ask questions? The only shady doctors I heard about as a cop are in jail for medical malpractice. I'd rather not have one that's had their medical license revoked for atrocities toward humans, if that's okay."

Eiji grinned. "Leave that to me. Though maybe you could define *atrocities toward humans*?"

Alec raised one eyebrow at Eiji. "Or animals, Eiji. Preferably not a veterinarian either."

The smaller Japanese vampire laughed. "Oh Alec, your lack of faith disturbs me. Anyway humans pay plastic surgeons good money for atrocities all the time." He grinned even wider. "But I can assure you, Alec, your family doctor knows more than you think."

Alec stared at Eiji, as did Cronin. "You know his family doctor?" Cronin asked.

Eiji nodded. "Of course. Alec saw him many times as a child. I needed to be certain the doctor was adequately qualified for Alec to be in his care."

"You what?" Alec asked.

Eiji rolled his eyes. "I couldn't have Cronin's fated one seen to by just anyone."

"THE DOCTOR WILL BE HERE at six tonight," Kole MacAidan said into the phone.

"Thanks, Dad. See you then." Alec clicked off the call

and threw the cell onto the table. "It's organized. Though Doctor Benavides thinks the house call is for my dad."

Jodis and Eiji were in the office going through the books they'd borrowed from the old library in Prague, giving Alec and Cronin some much needed privacy. Cronin put his forehead on Alec's shoulder and sighed. "I'm sorry you have to go through this," he murmured.

Alec put his hands to Cronin's face and lifted it so he would look at him. "It's not your fault. This isn't anyone's fault. It just is what it is. We had no way of knowing my blood would affect you like this. It's just a routine blood test and a physical."

Cronin growled again, a low petulant rumble. "What kind of physical?"

It made Alec laugh. "The kind you don't have to worry about." Alec looked at his new watch, then out to the beckoning sunrise. The wall of specially filtered glass protected the vampires within, without impeding the spectacular view of the city. "It's almost bed time," Alec said. "How about we start on our research before we call it a day."

Cronin nodded. "Where do you want to start?"

"I was making notes before," Alec told him. "Sometimes it helps to see the bigger picture when it's written in front of you." He found his notebook and read aloud what he'd written, the words Jorge had said.

From his blood comes the sun. Blood from a stone. Stone from a blood. So many questions. Blood from a stone.

Red hand, blue moon, silver river, the earth will come to life. Blood from a stone, stone from blood. He is risen already, as she was risen, the answer is in the stones. Blood from a stone, stone from a blood.

Cronin asked. "What does the key need to do?"

Blue moon, silver river, blood from a stone. You will not find him with your eyes.

Yes, through the key. Through the key.

Red hands in the stones. Forever is in the stones. The key asks different questions, he does. Yes, he does. Red hands in the stones. Forever is in the stones.

Alec was quiet for a moment as he thought it over. "He said the first part earlier. He said my blood comes from the sun when he was talking about the mummified vampires in Egypt. He saw that my blood resurrected Ra and the sun disk, killing all those poor souls. That's what he called them. He said they didn't know what they were doing, and he was right. Queen Keket never taught them, never fed them."

Cronin nodded. "He said it wasn't their fault. 'They knew not what they did.'"

"Yes, and I agreed with him. They needed to die, don't get me wrong, but it wasn't their fault. They were a product of their maker."

Cronin's black eyes flashed with memory. "And he said 'It wasn't the Queen who did wrong.'"

Alec nodded. "I assumed one of his personalities didn't like the fact that we killed so many vampires."

"Maybe." Cronin frowned. "He also said 'He is risen already, as she was risen.'"

"You think that was about Queen Keket?"

"It's hard to say for certain," Cronin answered. "His answers were hardly coherent, but we'd not talked about any other female vampire. Only Keket."

"'He is risen already, as she was risen.'" Alec repeated. "So whoever is plotting some evil plan this time around is already risen. Risen from the dead? Like a mummified vampire? Or just reborn as a vampire?"

"Risen to power?" Cronin offered. "It could mean anything. Or nothing."

"Or everything," Alec said. "And 'the earth will come to life.' Is he talking volcanoes, earthquakes? I can't be fighting natural disasters, for fuck's sake. Why can't the kid just work it out in his head before he speaks?"

Cronin laughed. "And which Jorge would you prefer to speak?"

Alec shivered as he remembered. "Preferably not the one with the black eyes."

Cronin feigned offense. "Is there something about black eyes you don't like?"

Alec laughed at him. "Your irises are black, yes, not your whole eyeballs. There's a difference. Yours are a fiery, smoldering black. His were dead, like a shark's."

"It is unnerving, yes?"

Alec nodded. "And as unnerving as it is, I think we need to see him again."

"I believe Jodis has spoken to Eleanor and asked her to visit," Cronin said. "We shall talk to her first and determine if she has seen anything of this new threat, without the riddles. She might be able to shed some light on Jorge's words."

Eleanor was a seer. A vampire with the talent of foresight. Not always accurate, and her visions could change on a whim, depending on decisions made and other outcomes, whereas Jorge's visions, although cryptic, were never wrong.

"And if we still need further clarification," Cronin continued, "then yes, seeing Jorge again makes sense."

"Maybe he can elaborate about all the stone references," Alec said. "Do you know what he meant by that?"

"Possibly."

"And the red hand? Silver river, blue moon. We think

we know what blue moon means, but what the hell does the rest of it mean?" Alec shook his head. "I'm too tired to figure this out."

Cronin took his hand. "Then rest. We can discuss theories after you've slept."

Alec studied Cronin for a long second. "What aren't you telling me?"

"Nothing, I—"

"Bullshit. I can tell." Alec pulled back his hand, leaned his ass against the dining table, and folded his arms. "Have I not told you everything?"

Cronin sighed. "Alec, I didn't want to worry you unnecessarily. I don't know if I'm even on the right track. Please don't be mad at me."

Alec knew his temper frayed easily when he was tired, and Cronin looked so sad that Alec's anger melted away. He almost forgot Cronin had experienced some transference of vampiric talents and that was weighing heavy on his mind. He opened his arms and invited Cronin into an embrace. "I'm not mad, but please don't think I'm some weak human who can't shoulder this with you." He cupped his hands to Cronin's face and kissed him. "Are we not in this together?"

Cronin almost smiled. "We are."

"Then tell me your theories," Alec said. "Tell me what you think Jorge was referring to about the stones."

"It wasn't the stones that concerned me," Cronin said. "It was the comment on the red hand."

Alec tried for some cryptic skew. "Some sort of communist mentality? There is the Irish reference to the red hand of Ulster. Could that be what he means? It's some Irish psychopath this time?"

Suddenly Jodis and Eiji were in the room, looking at them, clearly interested in their theories. "The Irish?"

Cronin simply shook his head. "I don't think so. The only vampire reference to a red hand I recall belonged to a vampire that lived eight hundred years ago. He also happened to live in the area now experiencing human disappearances."

"Who was it?" Alec asked.

Both Jodis and Eiji answered in unison. "Genghis Khan."

CHAPTER SIX

"GENGHIS KHAN?" Alec repeated. "As in *the* Genghis Khan, who ruled over Asia, China, and Europe? *That* Genghis Khan?"

Cronin nodded. "He claimed territories from as far east as Korea right across into Europe. He had faction covens, or generals as he called them, who claimed territories in his name for over a hundred years. It was an unprecedented carnage."

"Worse than the Black Plague?" Alec asked. He'd discovered a few months before that the Black Plague wasn't a plague as historians would have us believe, but a rogue coven of vampires who almost wiped out Europe in the 1300s.

"Much worse," Jodis said. "Millions of people died, Alec. Millions."

"And not just humans," Eiji added. "Any vampire who dared question his motive or authority met their fate also."

"You think it's him?" Jodis asked Cronin. She looked concerned now; her blue eyes swam with worry. "But how?"

"That, I don't know," Cronin answered. "That's what I

need to research. Jorge said *he is risen already*, and there have been reports of human disappearances in China and, more than likely, Mongolia. For us to hear reports or any news from these regions means it must be worse than they're letting on. And Kennard heard of southern Russian covens fleeing north." Cronin took a deep breath. "It makes geographical sense."

Alec pinched the bridge of his nose and exhaled slowly. "Genghis fucking Khan. Jesus Christ, you're serious aren't you?"

Cronin took his hand, making Alec look at him. "You should rest, Alec. You are tired."

Alec snorted. "You expect me to sleep now? And how would I ask the three hundred questions I have if I'm asleep?"

Cronin gave him a small smile. "I presumed you'd have questions."

"Um, yes. First one: how the hell was Genghis Khan a vampire and no one knows about it? And who else was a vampire that I should know about, over the course of fuck-ing-ever?"

Eiji laughed. "I do love the way you ask questions, Alec."

"Genghis Khan was a human boy named Temüjin," Cronin said. "It is believed a nomadic vampire slew Temüjin's village, including his father, the chief. When he was about eighteen, he was bitten but not killed."

"He gave himself an appointed title of Khan," Eiji said.

"Meaning ruler or king?" Alec asked. "I remember reading about him in high school. He was responsible for the Silk Road, postal services, communication, and currency, right?"

"He was responsible for a lot of things," Cronin said darkly.

"Did any of you guys meet him back then?" Alec asked.

The three vampires shook their heads, but it was Cronin who spoke. "No, we were not elders at that time."

Alec nodded. "Right. Because it was before the Black Plague attack that took out your elders."

Jodis nodded. "Yes."

"Okay," Alec nodded, finally getting his head around the absurdity of it all. "So what do you think he wants? What's the point of his return? And more importantly, how did he die the first time? If he was killed once, then we can kill him again, yes?"

"I don't know yet what he wants, or to what his return means. But do you mean how will the key bring an end to him?" Cronin asked rhetorically. "That's what I want to know also. That is what we need to find out."

Alec let his head fall back and he sighed loudly at the ceiling. "Who else is there?" Alec asked again. "Which other famous or infamous person throughout history am I likely to have to kill again? I mean, how many more are there? How long do I have to keep doing this?"

Cronin was quick to stand in front of him. He cradled Alec's face so gently, with so much love, it took Alec's breath away. He kissed Alec's cheeks, his eyelids, before pulling him against his chest. "I hate when you feel anguish, m'cridhe, for I feel it too."

Alec's voice was muffled by Cronin's shirt. "How am I supposed to fight this one?"

"We will figure this out together, Alec," Cronin whispered, kissing the side of his head. "You are not some weak human who has to shoulder this alone. Is that not what you said?" He kissed Alec softly. "I am forever by your side."

"As are we," Jodis said.

Finally, Alec smiled. "Just like the musketeers, huh? All for one and one for all."

Cronin pulled back a little so he could see Alec's face. "They weren't vampires."

"What about King Arthur?" Alec asked. Joking about it seemed to help with the overwhelming feeling. "Elvis?"

Eiji laughed. "No, and the rumors of Robin Hood are not true."

Jodis joined in. "No, he never wore that ridiculous hat."

Alec chuckled. "Let me guess, Santa Claus was a vampire who could leap. It would explain the ability to visit every child in the world in one night."

"I'm not sure a vampire would be inclined to give children gifts," Eiji said.

"No," Cronin agreed. "There's more truth in the legend of the Pied Piper than Santa Claus."

"The Pied Piper from the Nursery Rhyme?" Alec asked.

Jodis made a thoughtful face. "Yes. Don't discredit rhymes for children. There is often warning within each one."

"Oh, Jesus."

Cronin twisted his lips into a smile. He shook his head. "No. He wasn't one."

Jodis laughed. "The Pied Piper lived in Hamelin, Germany. This particular vampire preferred the blood of children. One hundred and thirty children, to be exact."

Alec's mouth fell open. "Children?"

"Yes," Cronin said quietly. "It is not an ethical practice, even for vampires, and he was brought to trial and executed in 1284."

"There was also Whitechapel," Eiji said. This time Cronin and Jodis both sighed.

"Whitechapel?" Alec clarified. "The Whitechapel murders? As in Jack the Ripper?"

Cronin nodded. "He was a particularly troubled vampire. He thought himself uncatchable."

"They never did catch him," Alec said. "Did they?"

"Not the police, no," Jodis said with an amused smile. "Kennard had the pleasure of putting an end to that little show."

Alec shook his head and puffed out a breath. "Jack the freakin' Ripper was a vampire?"

"Oh, yes," Cronin said. "Think about it, all crimes took place at night, the throats were cut to obscure bite marks. Though he liked to splash around in the blood. He really was rather peculiar."

Splash around in the blood? Cronin, Eiji, and Jodis all seemed to find that amusing, but Alec didn't. He put his hand up in a stop motion. "Yeah, okay that's enough. I don't think I need to know anymore." He sighed and looked out across the view of the city. It was now well and truly daytime. "I need to go to bed."

Alec only felt Cronin's arms slide around him before they were leaping. He landed on his back on Cronin's bed, with Cronin on top of him. "I could have walked from the living room," Alec said, unable to stop the smile.

"I know," Cronin replied. A soft purr became a low growl as he ran his nose along Alec's neck.

Then Jodis called out, "No feeding from Alec."

Cronin huffed out a frustrated growl, and Eiji laughed from three rooms away. Alec chuckled as well. "Shall we test your self-control?" he asked, biting his bottom lip. "Because I'm pretty sure you can fuck me and not bite me."

Cronin tore Alec's shirt from his body, making Alec laugh again. "I take it that's a yes."

CRONIN STAYED beside Alec in bed, both of them still naked, and watched Alec as he slept. He'd never imagined in all of his years that he'd have this. Not just a bedfellow, but his fated lover. Someone who was half of him, who filled his very heart and soul, who encompassed every thought.

Alec was everything he could have dared dream for. Perfectly designed just for him, he felt the fated bond in his bones. It was not something he could describe, when words were so inadequate. Not even the most distinguished of poets had words for this.

He took in Alec's human form, all defined muscles and strong lines, pale skin, smattering of hair in all the perfect places. His green eyes reminded Cronin of the moors of Scotland. His pink lips parted just so in breath. He also had trails of fang puncture marks on his neck and his inner thighs, markings Cronin should feel guilt for, yet only pride and possession filled him.

Alec was his, and he loved being bitten. He wore the bite marks with gratification, and he wanted other vampires to see, to know. And that pleased Cronin greatly.

Alec had been a little disappointed that Cronin had shown enough restraint not to bite him. It had taken a great deal of willpower not to sink his teeth into Alec's flesh, but he'd done it.

Cronin wondered whether this was also a first in vampire history, and if this now made him an incubus. He snorted to himself, causing Alec to stir in his sleep. Alec slid an arm around Cronin and nestled into him, encouraging Cronin's cock to fill. It didn't take much—a look, a touch, just being close—and Cronin's desire to have him flooded his body.

Despite only a few hours sleep, and only a few hours since their last joining, Alec seemed to sense Cronin's want. He stirred from his sleep again and moaned. It was a sound that made Cronin flex his hips. Without opening his eyes, Alec smiled and rolled onto his stomach. He spread his thighs and lifted his ass, moaning again.

Alec was still slick from their last time, filled with lube and come. Alec never wanted to be cleaned up. He loved that Cronin could release inside him, telling him time and again how good it made him feel. And Cronin loved it too. He loved that Alec would smell of him afterwards, that he'd laid claim to what was his, and made it his own, every time.

"Please," Alec murmured into the pillow. He arched his back and lifted his ass one more time.

Cronin never could say no to him.

He slid over Alec's back, lying between his spread thighs. Cronin's erection pressed against Alec's slick crack, and Alec whined underneath him until Cronin pressed his cock into him.

He slid in easily, and in one slow thrust he was fully seated inside him. Alec groaned louder this time, pushing his forehead into the pillow, and Cronin growled in his ear. Alec convulsed at the sound and cried out, lifting his ass the best he could, wanting everything Cronin would give him.

Cronin took Alec's hands and held them to the mattress above his head. He loved watching Alec's shoulder muscles bunch and slide under his skin, how the back of his neck would stretch as Alec pushed his forehead into the pillow.

He braced himself against Cronin's thrusts, giving himself so completely.

And Cronin took him.

He pushed in as deep as he could, being buried so far inside before pulling out and sliding back in as hard and deep as Alec's human body would allow. Pleasure soon took over and Cronin's thrusts became a little sharper, harder, and all he wanted to do was bite.

He wanted to sink his teeth through Alec's flesh as his cock sunk into his ass, he wanted to fuck and bite, to claim and to own. It was in his nature, it was a primal instinct, but his instinct to protect Alec was greater.

Cronin threw his head back, thrust once more, and came. Alec's body convulsed around him, gripping his cock and taking in every drop Cronin gave him. Cronin collapsed on top of Alec, sated and spent. Alec threaded his fingers with Cronin's to keep him right where he was, and before Cronin could even pull out of him, Alec was already fast asleep. Smiling and sated and, Cronin hoped, dreaming of pleasant things, he slept soundly.

A while later, when Alec's breaths had become soft snores, Cronin showered and went to speak with Jodis and Eiji who were in the office. They had books spread over the desk. Jodis sat in the chair, Eiji leaned against the desk. They both smiled at him when he walked in. "Have you found anything?" Cronin asked.

Eiji's smile became a grin and he went to say something, but Jodis stopped him. "I told him he's not to comment on your bedroom habits."

Cronin smiled, despite the personal subject matter. "I didn't bite him."

"We heard," Eiji said, and Jodis hissed at him, though she fought a smile. "Everything."

"Yes, I feel the need to apologize for the decades you endured with us in the early days," Jodis added, a faint blush tainting her alabaster cheeks. "I have no doubt you've suffered more than your share."

"Decades?" Cronin questioned. "What happened to centuries?"

"Yes, well," she amended with an embarrassed smirk. "Those too. I'm only now realizing how uncomfortable you must have felt."

"If you're uncomfortable—" Cronin started to say.

"Oh no, that's not what I meant," Jodis interjected quickly.

"Relax Jodis, my dear," Cronin said, now smiling. "I know what you meant."

Eiji laughed loudly. "I'm not apologizing for anything." He still wore a ridiculous grin. "Not for how loud we were, and not for the joking I'll do with Alec when he wakes up."

Cronin chuckled. "It's pleasing to see your good spirits keep company with good health, Eiji. I'm happy you're here and I know Alec is too. He's missed you both, despite Eiji's jokes at his expense."

"It's good to be back here with you too," Jodis said. "And to see you so happy, Cronin. I never realized you were so unhappy before you met Alec."

"I wasn't *un*happy," Cronin mused. "I don't think I knew what real happiness was. I was content with my life, as I knew it to be."

"And now?"

"And now I know why you would put up with Eiji all these centuries."

Eiji barked out a laugh and threw whatever it was he was holding at Cronin's head. He caught it easily and, still smiling, inspected it. It was a small metal filigree sphere

Cronin had collected from Italy a long time ago. Alec had been looking at it the other day and left it sitting on the desk when their conversations about the keepsakes he'd collected ended with them naked, as usual.

Cronin put it back on the shelf from where Alec had got it, and turned to face his friends. "I'm hoping you're going to tell me there's been a few human and vampire relations that ended favorably."

Jodis shook her head. "Nothing."

Cronin frowned. "I had an errant thought before, and I'm now wondering if there may be a vein of truth to the madness."

"What is it?" Jodis asked, concerned.

"Should we possibly look into the incubi?"

Eiji's eyebrows almost met. "What?"

"The ability to copulate without biting," Cronin said casually. "I just thought—"

"Cronin, no," Jodis said, standing up. She walked over to him and put her hand on his arm. "That's not what this is. This is not a manipulation, it's not coercion, it's fate."

"I know that," Cronin replied kindly. "But if we're looking at all possibilities. If we are to be objective, is it not in our best interest to examine such things?"

Jodis shook her head adamantly. Her eyes were a steely blue. "I can appreciate your logic, Cronin. It's generous of you to suggest the possibility, but I refuse to believe such a thing."

"As do I," Eiji said. "The incubi are deceitful, cruel even, and you are no such thing. What you and Alec have is real. You will share a bed and you will not feed from him because of the slightest chance of long-term effects on him, and you simply cannot cause him pain."

"I won't feed from him because of the effects it seems to be having on me," Cronin said weakly.

"Oh, give me some credit, brother," Eiji said with a laugh. "Do you not think after all these years I cannot read your face? As soon as Jodis mentioned effects on you, you looked at Alec, and I could see your mind tick over, Cronin. You thought if it could affect you, then it could affect Alec." Eiji gave a smug smile. "And you can't bear the thought of it, because you're *fated* to him. Not some incubus who would risk Alec's death for your own pleasure. Cronin, the notion is ludicrous."

Cronin sighed. "It was merely an errant thought."

Jodis gave him a sad smile. "Please disregard it." She looked at him for a long moment. "Cronin, we will find out what this all means. I promise."

"Which part?" he asked with a sigh. "The part where I've suddenly acquired the ability to transfer talents from other vampires? Or the part where I believe Alec has to go into combat against the greatest, most horrific conqueror the world has ever seen?"

Jodis' eyes softened. "My dearest friend, we will get through this. Though I will say, you are my immediate concern. Genghis Khan, if that is even who we are to face, can wait. This blue moon or the next, Cronin, it doesn't matter. Your well-being is my priority."

"And Alec's purpose in all this mess is mine," Cronin countered.

"Alec will have no purpose if you are compromised, Cronin," Jodis said. "If this change in you is not reversible, if there is no improvement now that you've stopped drinking his blood, then I don't know what that will mean. For either of you. Your fate is his as well. If you were to die, then he will follow...." Cronin growled softly and Jodis rephrased her point. "If you are compromised Cronin, then Alec won't be fighting anyone. We need to get you well first."

Cronin's brow furrowed at the thought. He hated putting Alec in jeopardy. He hated the mystery of it all. There were far too many questions and not enough answers. He looked over to Eiji. "Have you found anything in the medical books?"

"For various ways different human blood may affect a vampire?" Eiji clarified. "There's nothing which relates, in part, to you and Alec's relationship, and even if there was anything remotely close, there would still be too many variables. Cronin, you're the only vampire to ever feed repeatedly from the same source for any length of time. And there's never been a human key before, so it's a whole new level of unchartered territory. We simply have nothing to gauge this by."

"Maybe Alec's doctor appointment will uncover something," Jodis said.

Cronin nodded distractedly. "Yes. Speaking of which, Alec will be awake soon. I'd best start the coffee machine."

CRONIN LIKED ALEC'S FATHER. Kole MacAidan was a good man, so like his son albeit some twenty-odd years older. For the first thirty minutes of their visit, Alec sat with Kole on the sofa, talking of what had happened since their last conversation just a few days ago.

Cronin, on the other hand, sat on the recliner with Sammy the cat, who was purring so loudly both Alec and Kole kept glancing over at them.

Alec told his dad how they'd leapt to England and

Bolivia and how the newest development for the key may very well include Genghis Khan.

"Genghis Khan?" Kole repeated. "As in *the* Genghis Khan?"

Cronin chuckled. "That is exactly what Alec said."

"We're not a hundred percent sure yet, Dad," Alec added. "But what Cronin said makes sense."

"Jesus Christ," Kole hissed.

Alec smirked at Cronin before saying, "Well, I'm pretty sure Jesus won't be there, Dad."

"Oh har har, Alec. That's not funny." Kole shook his head. "And anyway, what's this doctor's appointment for? You boys are being safe, right?"

Cronin almost swallowed his tongue, whereas Alec just laughed. "Dad, please. I need to have my blood analyzed. We think it might have something in it that can affect vampires. We're not sure, but we just wanna check a few things out."

"I told you all along your blood was special," Kole said. He didn't seem surprised by any of this. He knew everything that Alec knew. He knew Cronin was a vampire, he knew he had some vampires on protective detail watching over him, and just like his son, took it all in stride.

"Mr. MacAidan," Cronin interrupted them. "Do you know anything else about his blood? You call it special, but do you know in which regard?"

"I take it this must be something important for you to be worried, but no, I'm sorry," Kole said. "Just that he was destined for great things. It was in his bloodline. That's all I know."

Cronin nodded. "It is important, yes. Thank you anyway." He paused for a long second. "This doctor knows of Alec's importance?"

"Albert ran tests on Alec when he was a boy. If he came off his bike or skateboard, he always healed fast, and Albert was curious," Kole told them. "He ran tests when he was, oh, about twelve. Said he had a high iron count, but everything else was perfectly normal."

"I've had dozens of blood tests and physicals," Alec added. "Nothing's ever been red-flagged before."

"You said it affects vampires?" Kole clued in on Alec's earlier choice of words. "You mean, it affects Cronin because he drinks it?"

Alec nodded. "Yes, Dad."

Kole looked at Alec, then at Cronin, and slowly back to his son. He was clearly shocked, and for the first time *ever*, Cronin felt guilt for what he was.

"Does it hurt?" Kole asked quietly.

Alec barked out a laugh. "Uh, no Dad. Quite the opposite, actually."

"Oh." Kole cleared his throat. "Right."

"I would never hurt him," Cronin said quietly.

"Hey," Alec said firmly, making Cronin look at him. "He knows that." He tilted his head just so, seemingly confused by what Cronin just said.

Cronin's cell phone buzzed in his pocket, and he was glad for the distraction. It was Jacques, the vampire who was given the duty of watching over and protecting Alec's father. Cronin had sent him a text to advise him that they'd be visiting so not to be alarmed. "Cronin, you have an incoming. Human, possibly sixty, he has a doctor's bag. Everything okay?"

"Everything's fine," Cronin answered. "Thank you. He is expected." Cronin clicked off the call to find Alec and Kole both looking at him. Then he heard a human heartbeat at the front door, and he looked toward it. "Your doctor friend has arrived." A moment later there was a sharp rap on the front door.

Alec stood up and held his hand out to Cronin. Putting a disgruntled cat on the floor, Cronin was quick to take the cue. Alec squeezed his hand. "You okay?"

"Of course. And you?" Cronin replied.

Kole gave them one glance over his shoulder before opening the door. He greeted the doctor and opened the door wider. "Albert. Please, come in."

"Kole," the doctor said. "You're not on my house call list. Everything alright?" He stopped talking when he saw Alec, and Kole shut the door. "Alec?"

Alec nodded. "Yes. And this is my partner, Cronin."

Doctor Benavides stopped in his tracks. He looked at all of them cautiously. "What's going on?"

"Sorry for the subterfuge," Kole said. "The appointment's not for me."

"You've seen the news, yes?" Alec asked. "You saw me do the disappearing thing on TV?"

The doctor nodded and eyed Cronin uneasily.

"Then you know I can't go to a hospital," Alec said. "I don't mean to implicate you, but I need your help. If you're not comfortable doing this or fear you'd be harboring a criminal, then you can walk out of here, no questions asked."

The doctor seemed to consider this for a moment. He looked at the three of them again, even glanced at the front door, but eventually looked Alec up and down. "What's the matter with you?"

Alec smiled at him. "Nothing's wrong exactly. I need blood tests done."

"What are you looking for?"

"Anomalies. I don't know exactly," Alec explained. "Something that wasn't there before."

The doctor blinked and rubbed his wrinkled hand over his face. His eyes were a grayish blue, his eyebrows were bushy and matched his salt and pepper hair.

Alec pulled a wad of neatly stacked bills from his jacket's inside pocket. "To cover any lab costs."

The doctor put his black bag on the dining table and sighed. "Put your money away, son." He looked around the room. "We okay to do this here?"

Alec grinned. "Sure." He took off his jacket and pulled out a chair, sitting in it. He laid his arm on the table and inspected the crook of his elbow and tapped the skin, searching for a vein.

Cronin took a deep breath.

When Doctor Benavides took a sterile pack of hypodermic needles from his bag, Cronin growled and took a step toward them. Kole was quickly in front of him with his hands to Cronin's chest, and he coughed to cover any inhuman sounds coming from Cronin. "Care to help me in the kitchen?" Kole asked, pushing Cronin toward the door.

Cronin could have easily stood his ground or knocked Kole through the wall if he wanted to—a human was no match for a vampire—but he knew Alec's dad was right, and he allowed himself to be ushered out the door. As he entered the small kitchen, he heard Alec say, "Uh, yeah, he's not a fan of needles."

"Whoa, Cronin, you with me, son?" Kole whispered. It was only then that Cronin realized Kole had his hands to Cronin's face. The man looked worried, and when Cronin swiped his fangs with his teeth, he realized why.

Cronin shook his head, trying to clear it.

"It's okay," Kole said softly. "He's not hurting him."

Cronin took a deep breath and realized that was probably not wise. The scent of Alec's blood filled his nose, his

CRONIN'S KEY II   71

throat, his senses. He wanted to taste it, and he wanted no one else to touch it. Every fiber in his body told him to kill the threat that touched his blood, his Alec. His body thrummed with danger and an energy he could barely contain. But he couldn't allow harm to come to Kole or his doctor friend.

He held his breath and shook his head again. His fangs wouldn't retract, the urge was getting too strong. "I can't be here," he said, his voice strangling in his throat.

Kole's eyes went wide. He seemed to understand and he nodded. "Go."

And Cronin leapt.

CHAPTER SEVEN

CRONIN CHANGED direction three times mid-leap, something he'd not ever done. He was so torn as to where to go, when all he wanted to do was to go back to Alec and tear the doctor apart for touching him.

His first thought was to go to the fields of Dunadd in Scotland, where he'd taken Alec many times, the field where his human life had ended. He'd found such peace there with Alec, but there would be no peace. Not without Alec.

Then he thought to go back to his apartment. Jodis and Eiji were there and they'd know what to say, what to do to calm him. But that wasn't what he wanted. He wanted to rage, to let out the anger and frustration, so found himself in the darkened streets of San Pedro Sula. Rife with crime, this city was easy pickings. Murderers, rapists, the city was infested with human maggots, and when Cronin leapt to a darkened alley, he didn't even have to look or listen. It was happening right in front of him. Two men held a struggling man down, face-first into the garbage-filled street. One held a knife to the back of his neck, the other was pulling his pants down. They noticed Cronin approach and they stopped, but before they could even speak, Cronin had them both by the throat, one in each hand.

The man on the ground scurried away and the two attackers kicked the air with their feet, a good ten inches off the ground. Cronin didn't waste a second. He threw one man into the alley wall, hard enough to render him unconscious. He grabbed the other man by the hair and violently tilted his head back, almost snapping his neck. He sunk his teeth into his throat, feeling the hot blood soothe his throat as he drank the life out of this man.

And when the first man was drained and lifeless, he let him fall to the ground like the garbage he was. Then, like he hadn't fed in weeks, Cronin picked up the second man and fed from him too.

But it didn't taste right. It wasn't rich enough, it wasn't sweet enough, it wasn't sustaining enough.

It wasn't Alec.

Alec.

And just like an answered prayer, Cronin heard him.

It's okay, Cronin. The doctor's nearly done. I'll see you soon.

Relief, coupled with shame, swept through him. Cronin picked up the two dead men by their throats and leapt.

Disposing of bodies was dependent on where it was still night somewhere around the world. Tonight's choice was one of his favorites.

Sunlight was almost breaking across the Serengeti, highlighting the plains of Tanzania in a spectacular mix of beauty and wild. He let the two bodies fall to the ground and stepped forward, smelling the air around him. His old friends were here, if that's what he could call them. He'd never brought anyone here, he'd never shared this secret with anyone. He knew he'd bring Alec here one day, though not while he was human. He wouldn't risk it. But yes, when Alec became a vampire, they would come here and they could marvel at it together.

Sometimes he'd discard of bodies in an ocean, or a ravine, or in the vast frozen lands of the arctic. Though the polar bears didn't appreciate the takeout like the lions of Tanzania did.

Cronin let his head fall back and he snapped out a roar. It was his calling card. He'd made that call for hundreds of years, and the pride knew his voice. As clear as someone chiming the dinner bell, the largest male lion appeared first.

What made cats attracted to vampires, Cronin could only guess. But a large lion thundered in to see him, nudging his hip before he sniffed out the closest body. Cronin ran his hand along the fine animal, feeling its coarse fur, feeling its strength as it walked, padding its huge feet in the dirt. As the light of the new day threatened to break over the horizon, the rest of the pride came in for the second body, and Cronin smiled with satisfaction as he leapt back to Kole's house.

He arrived in the kitchen and found Alec and Kole in the small living room. The doctor was, thankfully, gone. Alec stood up quickly and put his hand to the side of Cronin's face. "Are you okay?"

Cronin couldn't help it. He pulled Alec against him and breathed in his scent. "I am," he said. After a long moment, he turned to look at Alec's father. "I apologize for my behavior. I've not acted like that before."

"Like what?" Alec said. He pulled away but not too far. He looked worried. "Tell me what bothered you."

Cronin glanced at Kole and said, "Maybe it is a discussion best left for another time."

"Dad's okay with everything," Alec said. "He gets it, Cronin. He does."

Cronin sighed. "My whole body objected to someone else taking your blood. I could barely contain it. I wanted to kill him."

"But you didn't," Kole said. "And that's all that matters."

Alec looked concerned, but he tried to smile. "So where did you go?"

"To feed the lions of Tanzania," Cronin replied.

Kole laughed as if Cronin had made a joke, but Alec eyed him curiously. Before he could say anything, Cronin said, "I heard you again."

"Did you?" Alec asked. "I wondered if you would. I think Doctor Benavides thinks I'm crazy. I spoke to you like you were right there, but I'd hoped you'd hear me."

"It was grounding and most appreciated, thank you." Cronin didn't think Alec knew just how much he needed to hear his voice in that particular moment. "What else did the doctor say?"

"We'll have results in forty-eight hours." Alec held out his arm where a bandage held a cotton swab in place. "It took no time at all. And my physical was fine—"

Cronin growled again. "I don't think it prudent to be telling me of him touching you right now."

Alec kissed him with smiling lips. "It's not like he gave me a prostate exam." Cronin's growl got louder, and Alec laughed. "You ready to go?"

Cronin turned to Kole. "Again, I apologize. Thank you for being so understanding."

"No problem," he replied. "Be sure to let me know whatever you find out. If I can be of any help, just let me know."

"Thanks, Dad. I'll see you again soon," Alec said. Then

he slid his arm around Cronin's waist. "Take me home and cook me breakfast."

Cronin smiled. "Your wish, my command."

CRONIN HAD BECOME QUITE adept at cooking omelets with ham and peppers. The texture was repulsive, the smell offensive, but Alec would moan with every mouthful, and that alone was worth it.

As Alec finished his meal, Cronin told Eiji and Jodis about the visit with the doctor. "I've not experienced anything like it," he said. "It was a jealousy and anger like I've not felt before."

Jodis darted out of the room only to come back in with one of the books we'd taken from Prague. She had it opened to a particular page. "I found this. Fifth century Romania there was a vampire who was unable to feed. Her face was badly disfigured in her human death, and her change to vampire somehow resulted in no fangs. The one who changed her took pity upon her and would gather the blood in a bowl for her to drink from. It worked for some time, then he decided it would be easier to keep a human and bleed them as needed."

"The vampire repeatedly fed from the same source," Cronin concluded.

Jodis nodded. "Yes."

"The ill effects?"

"None," Jodis said. "She lived for another hundred years."

Cronin was disappointed. He wanted answers. It would somehow be easier to learn this poor woman vampire had gone mad.

"You want to know what I think?" Eiji asked. "I think you're reading too much into it. Your behavior today toward that doctor was understandable, Cronin. Alec's your mate. Believe me, if someone tried to take anything from my Jodis, I would want to kill them too."

"It was the taking of his blood that bothered me," Cronin added.

"Even more reason to be possessive," Eiji said simply. "Vampires are territorial over a human they're feeding from, let alone one they're fated to."

Cronin didn't particularly care for Eiji's phrasing, but he understood the sentiment. "So this is normal?"

"There is no *normal* in this scenario," Eiji said with a smile. "Just what's understandable or not surprising, at the very least. Cronin, Alec's blood is different. It's special. We know that. There's been no other blood like it that we know of or, if there was, that human wasn't a key to the vampire world. The fact that he is both is unsurpassed, or maybe his special blood is the very reason he is the key. Cronin, we have no way of knowing. But I think Jodis is right. As long as you stop drinking it, you'll be fine."

"I do not wish to stop drinking it," Cronin admitted quietly. He looked at his two dearest friends and lowered his voice so there was no way Alec could hear. "I fed off two humans today and I still want more."

Just then, Alec walked into the living room carrying a whiteboard. "Time to get to work," he announced. "Much to do, much to do." He set the whiteboard up on the table and wrote down some points of what he knew so far: disappearances in China and Mongolia and coven relocations.

Then he wrote down Jorge's cryptic words of silver river, blue moon, red hand, blood and stone, and when he turned around, he saw the three vampires were watching him. He clapped his hands together. "Come on, look alive you lot. We have work to do."

Jodis smiled and collected her book before standing up. Eiji laughed and said, "You're bossy for a human." They were still smiling as they disappeared toward the office.

And all Cronin could do was smile at him. Alec simply grinned back as though he didn't have a care in the world. He collected his laptop and threw himself onto the sofa beside Cronin, putting his feet on the coffee table and scanning internet sites on Genghis Khan. He jotted down points of interest and dates into his small notebook while Cronin was supposed to be reading Chinese news sites for anything of interest. He wasn't really. He was watching Alec.

"Are you just gonna watch me all day?" Alec said, not looking up from his laptop screen.

"I was thinking I would, yes," Cronin replied. "I like watching you do your detective thing. It's fascinating."

Alec snorted. "Fascinating?"

"Yes, the cognitive leaps your mind makes are remarkable."

Alec raised one eyebrow. "Leaps? I think your version of leaping is enough for both of us."

"Not that kind of leaping," Cronin said, amused. He leaned in and whispered, "Though I could leap us to bed if you'd so prefer."

Alec laughed and playfully pushed Cronin's shoulder. "Work, remember? We have a new psycho vampire to stabilize, if you recall."

"Stabilize?"

Alec grinned. "It's the politically correct way to say kill an enemy."

"Tell me what you have so far," Cronin said.

"Well, I only know what human history tells me of

Genghis Khan, but as you guys said the other day, the numbers of deaths by his hand or in his name were staggering. He was very powerful and his power of persuasion must have been even more so. Or, persuasion was his literal vampire talent. Is there any way we can check that?"

Jodis and Eiji were suddenly in the room. Alec was getting used to their vampire speed. "The talent of influencing another vampire's behavior is called manipulation," Jodis said. "A manipulator is not welcome in any coven. In more cases than not, they are killed as newborn vampires, quite often by the one who made them. They cannot be controlled and come to power quickly."

"Could Khan have been a manipulator?" Alec asked again. "From a profile study, I'd say it fits the bill." He didn't wait for an answer. He stood up and walked to the whiteboard and wrote 'manipulator' under the name Genghis Khan. Then he circled the word blood and did the same to the word stone.

"So," he went on to say. "Blood, we assume is mine. But stone," he tapped the whiteboard with the marker. "What does stone mean? And what does it mean for Genghis Khan."

"The Great Wall of China is constructed of it," Jodis offered.

"True," Alec said. "Though how does that relate to vampires? Are they buried in it?"

"No," Eiji said. "It was constructed by humans in a vain attempt to keep vampires from crossing into their lands."

"Hmm," Alec frowned. "Well, clearly they weren't too bright."

Cronin snorted out a laugh. "Not impressed by a constructional wonder of its time?"

Alec shrugged. "Don't get me wrong. I mean the wall

itself is a masterpiece, but not for the purpose of keeping vampires out...." He frowned again, as he obviously thought of something, and stared out the glass wall as he collected his thoughts. "Of course!"

He dashed to his laptop and tapped the keyboard, bringing up several tabs at once. "Why didn't I think of this before? You told me in the beginning," he said looking right at Cronin. "It makes perfect sense."

"What makes sense?" Cronin asked.

"Pyramids. You told me in the beginning when we were dealing with the Egyptian vampires, there are burial pyramids all over the world, including China."

The three vampires stared at him, waiting for him to piece it all together.

"Now the Chinese government has kept these pretty quiet, but there are a few photographs of the Chinese pyramids leaked to the outside world. But tying these clues together—Khan, the Shaanxi province, pyramid, and stone have to mean something." He typed in a few more words and waited for the internet searches to come up. His face went pale, drained of all color. "Oh fuck."

"Alec, what is it?" Cronin asked.

Alec turned the laptop around to show them all. On the screen was Mount Li. A seemingly inoffensive tree-covered hill in the green fields of Shaanxi province, China.

"Mount Li," Alec said. "Mount Li was a pyramid. It looks like a hill now, but two thousand years ago, it was a pyramid. If they'd built it out of stone like the Egyptians did, it'd still be standing today. It's a fucking pyramid, bigger than anything the Egyptians ever did. It has a tomb and everything."

Cronin stared at him. "Of course. And the reference Jorge made to earth *coming to life* wasn't about the Earth or volcanoes or earthquakes. He was referring to earth, as in terra."

Alec paled. "Terracotta."

"The Terracotta Army," Eiji whispered.

Alec nodded mechanically as realization sunk in. "The Terracotta Army will come to life."

CHAPTER EIGHT

"IS THERE anything else you guys'd like to tell me?" Alec asked. "We've been through the famous people in history who were vampires, but what about armies of vampires buried in the ground? Are there any more? The Egyptians, now the Chinese. Anyone else I should know about?"

"Well, there are Aztecs in the Tenochtitlan pyramids," Cronin said.

"And the pyramid of Cholula in Mexico is one of the biggest pyramids in the world for a reason, so...." Jodis added.

"There is still much human debate over whether the Visoko pyramid in Bosnia is even a pyramid," Eiji said.

The three vampires all laughed.

Alec rubbed his temples and he sighed, long and loud. "You know what? I don't even want to know." He stared at the whiteboard for a while and reluctantly wrote Terracotta Army under Genghis Khan. He shook his head at how absurd it all was. "How the hell am I supposed to kill six thousand terracotta soldiers?"

Cronin was beside him in a second with his hands

cupping his face. "With us. We will figure it out, but please know Alec, you are not in this alone."

"The Terracotta Army are vampires," Alec said quietly. "How is that even possible?"

"A mason," Jodis said.

"No shit." Alec rolled his eyes. "I'd say it took a thousand masons."

Jodis smiled at him. "No, I mean a mason, as in a vampire with the talent to turn things to stone."

Alec's mouth fell open and he blinked. And he blinked again. "A what?"

"There aren't too many of them these days," Eiji added. "But the vampire who turned the Terracotta Army to stone lived even before my time."

Cronin pulled Alec against him and Alec melted. Overwhelmed by what he'd just learned, Alec allowed himself to be held, to be protected, cradled by arms that made him feel safe and warm. "The Terracotta Army aren't technically stone," he mumbled.

"Maybe the mason could use the earth or clay instead of stone like how I can use water to turn to ice," Jodis explained. "No talent is an exact science."

"What other talents are there?" Alec asked. "I asked this before, but I mean the other ones. There are seers, leapers, and Eiji does his DNA lifespan thing, and Jodis can turn stuff into ice. Keket could regenerate the dead, it seems maybe Genghis Khan can influence the behavior of others. You mentioned mind-reading but they usually go mad. So what other ones haven't I heard of?"

"There are pyrokinetics, or fire starters," Cronin said.

"Like the guy in London?" Alec asked. "At the bar."

Cronin gave a nod. "Yes."

"Hydrokinetics can control water," Jodis said.

"Like you," Alec pressed.

She smiled. "Similar, but not the same. What I can do is called cryokinesis."

"There are some who can manipulate the air."

"Like that cartoon with the little guy with the blue arrow on his head who's an airbender."

The three vampires stared at him. No one spoke.

"Never mind."

"There are some who can influence what a human will hear," Cronin went on to say. "Like bells or a telephone, or a voice."

"So when you think you've heard someone call your name but when you look there's no one there?" Alec asked. "That's a vampire?"

"Yes."

"There are some who can control what you smell," Eiji said. "A whiff of perfume or the smell of food cooking."

"That's a vampire?" Alec shivered.

Jodis gave a nod. "It is to lure prey. A human might go looking for the source."

"There are also replicators, or doppelgängers, as humans would say," Cronin said quietly. "Though they are usually executed soon after they're changed."

Alec was stunned. He stared at Cronin with wide eyes. "Executed?"

"During the changing process, a vampire who will become a replicator changes many times repeatedly, taking forms of most of the people they'd met during their human life," Eiji said. "The vampire who changed them usually end it before the transformation is complete."

"Why?"

"They can replicate any form, human or vampire. They can assume identities, pretending to be anyone they come into contact with," Jodis said. "It's far too dangerous a talent. They could become Cronin and you would not know."

Alec swallowed hard. "What if... what if I become a replicator? What happens when I become a vampire, if that's my talent? Do you have to kill me?"

Cronin's arms tightened protectively around him and shook his head. "No. I would hide you and we would teach you how to control it." Cronin spoke with such quiet determination, with such reverence, Alec could not doubt him. "I wouldn't let anyone touch you."

After a moment of silence, Alec asked, "Are there any others? Other talents?"

"The Greek believed the god Morpheus influenced dreams," Jodis said. "But there are some who can influence the sleeping mind."

"The Japanese also claimed a demon named Baku would steal dreams," Eiji added. "But we know it was no demon. The purpose of this talent is not really known. Maybe there is no purpose."

"To influence," Alec said, pulling away from Cronin so he could look at everyone. "My father said both he and my mom had the same dream the night before I was born."

Cronin's brow furrowed. "Yes, he did." He looked to Jodis and Eiji. "To influence the name he was to be given. Ailig was a chosen name."

"Chosen by who?" Alec asked. "Why was my name important?"

"Ailig means defender of humankind, yes?" Jodis asked. "So someone knew, even before your birth, that you were the key?"

With his usual smile gone, the look of worry on Eiji's face seemed so out of place. "Your father said generations before him knew your bloodline was special." He held out his hand. "Alec, if I may?"

"If you may what?"

"Can I read you again," Eiji clarified. "Come sit on the sofa, this might take a while."

Alec begrudgingly left the warmth of Cronin's embrace and sat down beside Eiji. He gave him a smile. "If you just wanted to hold my hand, you only have to ask." Cronin growled from across the room. Alec held out his other hand, inviting Cronin to take it. "You can have this one."

Cronin snarled but he took the offer, sitting on the other side of Alec.

"You really don't like anyone else touching him, do you?" Jodis asked. She looked amused, but there was a hint of something in her eyes that Alec couldn't quite place. Confusion? Disbelief?

Cronin frowned. "No."

Eiji didn't seem too fazed. He just smiled at Alec and asked, "Remember when you adamantly told him he didn't own you?"

Alec rolled his eyes. "Shut up."

Eiji laughed then settled in to do his DNA reading thing. From just a touch, Eiji caught a glimpse of heredity, both past and future. Alec really had no clue how it worked, only that Eiji could see lifespans at a touch. Only this time, he was holding his hand much longer, as though he was trying to see something he hadn't seen before. Then Eiji frowned. "Cronin, let go of his hand."

Cronin did as he was asked, and Alec couldn't help but ask, "Why?"

Eiji didn't answer. He closed his eyes, concentrating on whatever it was he saw in his mind. "That's better," Eiji said, then after another few seconds he let go of Alec's hand. He looked at Cronin. "Could you see any of that?"

Cronin shook his head. "No. What's going on, Eiji?"

"I thought I'd look at his family history, to see if his ancestors, who knew about this special bloodline, were prominent. To be honest, I've only concentrated on his future. We wanted to know if he'd be vampire, if he'd live a long life. I never paid too much attention to his past."

"Eiji," Cronin growled out. "Explain, please."

"When you were holding his hand, I saw both of you," Eiji said. "It was very strange."

"Both? How is that possible?" Jodis asked.

Eiji shrugged. "I don't know. Can you hold his hand, please?" he asked her. "I'll see if it works the same."

When Jodis took Alec's hand, Cronin seemed too concerned about what was going on to be worried that someone else was touching Alec. He never took his eyes off Eiji. "What do you see?"

"Both," he answered. Eiji looked at Alec and shook his head. "Like you're some kind of conductor."

"What...?" Alec was dumbfounded. He looked to Cronin. "What does that mean?"

"I don't know," Cronin said. He looked a little bewildered.

Jodis said, "Alec, touch Cronin's leg." Then, still holding Alec's other hand, she closed her eyes.

"Jodis," Cronin hissed out a warning.

Jodis looked to Alec. "Did you feel that?"

"Feel what?"

Cronin's eyes went wide. "You didn't feel that?"

Alec shot up off the sofa. "Feel what? What the fuck is going on?"

Cronin was quickly in front of Alec, standing between

him and Jodis and Eiji. He put his hands to Alec's chest and up to his neck. "Jodis sent a burst of ice through you to me. It should have affected you, you should have felt it at least."

Alec shook his head and spoke in a whisper, "What does any of this mean? Cronin, what's happening to me?"

Cronin slid his hand around Alec's neck and pulled him against him. "I don't know."

"Uh, Cronin?" Eiji interrupted. "When I read his past, I didn't see anything. His father and paternal grandfather, grandmother, yes. But when I looked for his ancestors past that, there weren't any."

Just then, before anyone could question what Eiji had just said, Jodis' phone rang. She spoke into the cell, fast and low, and disconnected the call. "Eleanor is here. She's on her way up."

ELEANOR WAS the seer who had helped them with their battle against Keket in Egypt. She was an older woman, at least sixty in human years, an age not typical in vampires, but she was also blind. Well, her eyes were milky, clouded over, yet she saw with her mind. She saw things that could change and therefore may never happen, and sometimes she saw merely snippets, so her gift wasn't exact. But it was helpful, nonetheless.

"It's good to see you again," Alec said.

She took his hands in hers. "And you, Ailig. Busy again, I see?"

Alec snorted. "Well, trouble seems to find me. What can I say? I bring out the best in people."

Cronin didn't even have to speak. She turned and faced

him, and bowed her head slowly, respectfully. "Cronin, you are troubled."

"I have concerns, yes," he replied.

"You have been drinking gifted blood, I see," she said. Her white eyes flickered as she searched for things only she could see. "Hmm, interesting."

"What do you see?" Jodis asked.

"It has a transferring effect, yes?" she asked.

"We believe so," Cronin answered. "We were hoping you could tell us more. What do you see of it?"

"I see it has ill-effects," she replied. Cronin nodded, but she corrected him. "Not on you, Cronin, but on Alec."

What? "No, I feel fine. Actually, I feel great." Alec shook his head. "I've never felt this good."

"What do you see?" Cronin demanded of her.

"I see Alec is not well. He is fallen and ill," she said gently. "It will take a great deal to save him, but he will live."

"What? Where? When?" Cronin barked. His Scottish accent was always more pronounced when emotions were high. As was his proper speech. "Speak of all you see!"

"This battle you fight," she said. "I can't see what it is, Cronin. The air is too thick."

"What does that mean?" Eiji asked.

Eleanor shook her head. "Let me sit a while and concentrate," she said. She walked directly over to the sofa like she could see just fine and sat. She took a deep breath and closed her eyes. It was almost like a meditation. Her head swayed a little, and the four standing people in the room stared and waited.

"There are four divisions," she said. "He's waiting for the fifth." She opened her eyes. "He's waiting for Alec. He knows you will come."

"Who is he?" Cronin demanded. "Enough riddles!"

"Genghis Khan," she answered. "But you knew that. You all knew that already."

"I'm the fifth division?" Alec asked. His head was beginning to swim. "Of what?"

"What he needs to win, Alec," Eleanor explained. "You are the key to his success, as much as you are the key to yours."

"Meaning?" Cronin roared. He was clearly out of patience.

"As he was with Keket. She needed you to bring back Osiris, but it was your blood that bought back Ra to kill her," Eleanor said. "Khan needs you to win whatever war he's waging, Alec. But it is also your blood—when used against him—that will see him undone."

Alec walked mechanically over to the sofa across from Eleanor and dropped himself into it. He rubbed his temples. His voice sounded tired and resigned, even to his own ears. "The five divisions of what?"

"I don't know," she said softly. "I cannot see."

"When?"

"Soon. This full moon."

"Do I get sick before we go or when I'm there?" Alec asked quietly.

"When you are there," she answered. "But the damage is already done."

"What damage?" Eiji asked.

Eleanor swayed some more, searching her mind, before she shook her head. "I can't see it. Something is clouding, hiding what is meant to be. His blood is too powerful, though. Is it possible a human cannot contain it?"

"But he cannot be changed," Cronin said. He sat down next to Alec taking his hand, but he spoke to Eleanor. "You said after Egypt, his blood as the key was needed one more time, then he could be changed."

"Yes," Eleanor said. "That remains so."

Jodis shook her head. "But if he can't be human to survive, and he can't be changed...?"

"It will be close," Eleanor said. "But Alec will be a vampire. He will get his forever."

Alec snorted. "It's just gonna be a helluva ride, huh?"

Cronin was still staring at Eleanor. He frowned. "Why did you say that?" he asked. "We saw Jorge and he said something similar."

"If you spoke to Jorge, I don't see what I can tell you," Eleanor said incredulously. "His gift is much stronger than mine."

"Because he speaks in riddles, that's why," Alec told her. His tone was short and clipped, mirroring his patience. "We thought you might be able to shed some light on what the hell was going on. First we get news of a new enemy, which we figured out was Genghis Khan—with no help from Jorge, mind you—then Cronin starts to transfer gifts of other vampires because my blood is fucked up. And we need answers, not cryptic clues." He took a deep breath. "So please, anything you can tell us. Anything at all."

"The talent transfer is alarming," Eleanor said. "Fascinating and powerful, but alarming. Alec, I can't wait to see what powers you will yield when reborn as a vampire."

"Can you not see that?" Alec asked.

Eleanor shook her head. "No. There is no knowing until it occurs. Though you will be powerful. How can you not be? A human key that will become vampire? I'd imagine very powerful indeed."

Cronin, Eiji, and Jodis all looked at Alec and each of them smiled a little proudly. "I don't want to be powerful,"

Alec said, shaking his head. "I just want peace and fucking quiet and no psycho vampires vying for world domination to have to kill."

Eiji laughed and Alec glared at him. He wasn't in the mood. "I'm being serious, Eiji."

The Japanese vampire laughed again. "I know, that's what makes it so funny."

Cronin squeezed Alec's hand and steered the conversation back to Eleanor. "Jorge said forever was in the stones. What do you think he meant?"

"Tell me everything he said," Eleanor said.

Cronin repeated verbatim, what Jorge had said.

From his blood comes the sun. Blood from a stone. Stone from a blood. So many questions. Blood from a stone.

Red hand, blue moon, silver river, the earth will come to life. Blood from a stone, stone from a blood. He is risen already, as she was risen, the answer is in the stones. Blood from a stone, stone from a blood.

Blue moon, silver river, blood from a stone. You will not find him with your eyes.

Yes, through the key. Through the key.

Red hands in the stones. Forever is in the stones. The key asks different questions, he does. Yes, he does. Red hands in the stones. Forever is in the stones.

"We think we understand some of it," Alec said. "The blue moon, of course, and 'blood comes from the sun' comment is what happened in Egypt. The earth coming to life is the Terracotta Army, we think, and the part about them being risen, we have figured out. But blue moon, silver river, red hand, blood from a stone we have no clue. If he means stone as in terracotta, we just don't know. There's a saying that to get blood from a stone is impossible, so does he just mean we do the impossible? Is it that simple?"

"It could be," Jodis answered. "But I don't think it likely. Nothing Jorge says is simple."

"Nor should it be disregarded," Eiji added. "If he said it, it means something."

Eleanor frowned and her head swayed back and forth as though she was searching through her mind for the answers. "Forever is in the stones," she repeated, mumbling to herself. "I see you all underground. I see a large room, there are terracotta vampire soldiers and horses—"

Alec interrupted. "There are vampire *horses*?" He blinked slowly. "What the actual fuck?"

Eleanor shook her head. "They did not fare well with the change."

Alec put his hands up. "Okay, stop." The four vampires stared at him. "Horses? As in equine, My Little Pony, clippety-clop fucking horses?"

Cronin squeezed his hand. "Animals do not change, at least, not well. There have been some attempts at vampiring guard dogs, but the animal—" He made a face. "—does not complete well." He looked at Eleanor. "These horses were turned to terracotta over two thousand years ago, yes?"

She nodded. "Perhaps those who did it didn't know, or perhaps they hoped in vain. The Mongols revered their horses. They still do. They are a country forged on horseback. It's not pleasant, but I am not surprised to see horses in tombs alongside their soldiers."

Alec shivered from head to foot, and Cronin let go of his hand so he could put his arm around him. "Alec, are you well?"

He gave Cronin a weak smile and nodded, then looked back at Eleanor. "I interrupted before, sorry. Do you see anything about stones?"

Eleanor closed her eyes again and was quiet for a

moment. She took a deep breath and her eyes flew open. "There is a stone. I see it. It's a stone plate. There are inscriptions on it and a maze patterned into it. It is well-guarded." She shook her head quickly. "It is where Alec will fall."

Cronin growled, a low rumbling sound, as though the mere mention of harm to Alec was a threat. "Then we won't go. Let someone else kill him."

"Don't I have to?" Alec asked him. "Isn't that the point of being the key?"

Cronin stared at him, his eyes a feral onyx. "I won't risk you."

"If he doesn't fulfill his purpose," Eleanor said. Her eyes were closed again, her head swaying. "He will die a human."

"He needs to do this so he can be changed?" Jodis asked.

Eleanor sighed deeply. Her eyes opened. "It appears so. I cannot see why, only that it is."

"Something must happen to him when he falls," Eiji said. "Something must happen to his blood, to change whatever it is that makes it special."

Alec slumped against Cronin. The thoughts of this were weighing him down. "I survive though, right?" he asked.

Cronin made a low whining sound that was almost like a cry. He tightened his hold on Alec and kissed the side of his head. "I hate that you must endure this."

Alec sat up straight and pulled back a little so he could look into Cronin's eyes. "I know you do. But Cronin, it doesn't matter what I have to go through. As long as I get you forever, then it'll all be worth it."

"It seems every turn for answers only gives us more

questions," Cronin said quietly. "Jorge talked of questions. It seems even he could see everything we face is unanswered."

Eiji sat down next to Eleanor. "Can you see how we kill the Terracotta Army?"

Eleanor gasped and shot up from the sofa. The look on her face was one of fear. "They're coming. Now. Go! Get Alec somewhere safe!"

Before Alec could even blink, two Chinese warrior vampires appeared in the living room, their faces etched in anger, their fangs bared. They spoke in Chinese, wielded wooden spears, and lunged toward him.

CHAPTER NINE

LEAPERS. Chinese warrior vampires with the ability to leap from one place to the next, just like Cronin, whirled wooden spears above their heads. Dressed in red with black leather chest plates, they moved in unison, synchronized in violence as they swung their spears.

Alec barely saw Eiji and Jodis react before Cronin had his arms around him and they were gone.

Hit by a blast of winter air, Alec found himself in complete darkness, his back pressed against a stone wall and Cronin at his front. His heart hammered so damn fast he thought it might actually stop.

Alec recognized this place immediately. It was the Hill-fort at Dunadd, where Cronin had lived his human life. It was long abandoned and completely exposed to the Scottish elements, but it was remote and private, and obviously the first place Cronin thought of when he thought of the word *safe*.

Alec sucked back a breath. His heart was pounding and his adrenaline was pumping. "Eiji! And Jodis! We need to go back!" he said. "We can't leave them there!"

"There are no two more adept fighters," Cronin said. He put his hands to Alec's face and scanned his features, and even in the dark, Alec could see how wide and black his eyes were. "Are you hurt?"

Alec shook his head. "No. Cronin, we can't leave them!"

"I needed to get you out of there."

"They knew where we were!"

Cronin nodded. "We will need to move."

"What the hell did they say?" Alec asked. "They yelled something in Chinese."

"It wasn't Chinese. It was Mongolian. They said, 'In the name of Genghis Khan!'"

Alec shivered. The instant change, from a climate controlled New York apartment to a blustery Scottish night-filled field, was more than a shock. Not to mention the fright he'd just had. His whole body shuddered and his teeth chattered. "We need to go back, please Cronin. I can't leave them."

"And if there are now a hundred assassins in that room?" he retorted. "I cannot risk you being there!"

"If there are a hundred assassins in that room, then we need to go back now!"

Just then, Cronin's cell phone beeped. He fished it out of his pocket and read the screen. "It's a message from Jodis," he said, and Alec sighed in relief. "It says 'sikre.'"

"Is that some kind of code?"

"Yes," Cronin said flatly. "It's Norwegian for secure. She's telling us it's safe to go back."

Alec's teeth were still chattering. "Okay."

"Are you ready?"

Alec nodded, and they were gone.

ALEC FOUND himself in their bedroom. The light was on and bright compared to the darkness he'd just been in, but at least it was warm. He was still shivering, his teeth chattering and whole body covered in gooseflesh.

Cronin listened for one second then seemed to relax just a little. He grabbed Alec's hand and led him out into the living room. Jodis had her phone to her ear, talking in a language Alec didn't know. Eiji was dropping the bullet-proof vests and left over weapons from their last fight in Egypt onto the sofa. Eleanor stood by the wall, which used to be the glass wall that overlooked the city but was now the metal security wall. And two long wooden spears lay haphazardly amongst a spray of brown dust on the white marble floor.

"Thank you, Eleanor," Cronin said.

She looked a little shaken, even for a vampire. "I am sorry I didn't see it sooner. They must have a cloaker, Cronin. Someone is hiding their actions."

Eiji stuffed arrows into a backpack. "We need to leave," he said without looking up.

Cronin gave a hard nod. "Agreed."

"What about my dad," Alec asked. "If they found us, then they must know of him."

Cronin squeezed Alec's hand before letting it go. He put his phone to his ear and quickly spoke to someone in French, then redialed and spoke in English. "Kole, it is Cronin. Jacques will be at your door. Please let him in. You need to come with us. Alec and I will be there directly to get you both."

From what Alec could understand, his father mustn't

have argued. Cronin put his phone in his pocket. "Alec, you will need two jackets."

Alec raced into the closet and grabbed two jackets, one for him and one for his dad. When he came back out, Cronin was helping Eiji pack stakes and pistols into backpacks. Alec threw the jackets on the sofa. Cronin simply announced they wouldn't be gone long and slid his arm around Alec, and they leapt.

WHEN ALEC and Cronin landed in Kole's living room, Kole was at the front door with Jacques. Alec's father, a gray-haired man almost in his sixties, was wide-eyed and pale. "Dad?" Alec rushed to him. "You okay?"

Kole nodded weakly. "Yeah, yeah. I'm just too old for this middle of the night crap."

Cronin wasted no time. "Kole, do you have a book on your family history? Any documentation you may have would be greatly appreciated."

Kole nodded and darted out of the room.

Alec noticed then that his dad was wearing pajamas. "I'll go throw some clothes in a bag," Alec said, following his father down the hall. He heard Cronin ask Jacques if he'd seen anything out of the ordinary while he watched over Kole, but he didn't hear Jacques' reply. He stuffed handfuls of clothes into a small overnight bag and when he went back to the living room, Kole was already there.

He was holding a book Alec had never seen. "I only have this one...." His words died away.

Cronin was holding a pamphlet out to Kole. He looked pissed or worried, possibly both. "Where did you get this?"

"Uh, it's funny you should mention that," Kole answered quietly. "I got a phone call from some guy at Discovery Times Square who said I won tickets. I didn't believe him, you know, those marketing phone calls are a pain in the ass. But he said random winners were picked from their state library card numbers. He quoted my number.... Then there was that in my mailbox. I put the tickets on top of the fridge."

"What is it?" Alec asked.

Cronin handed Alec the piece of paper and walked into the kitchen. Alec read the flyer, and needles of ice and fear ran down his spine. The hair on the back of his neck stood on end.

There, on letterhead of the museum, was a letter addressed to his father. "Mr. MacAidan, the Terracotta Army has waited two thousand years to see you."

Cronin walked back in with the tickets in his hand. His jaw was set, his eyes were a steely black. Without a word, he put his hand on Alec, Alec put one hand on Jacques, and before he could touch his father, Kole cried, "Wait!"

He ran back down the hall and came back out with Sammy the cat tucked under one arm. "Can't just leave him here to starve," Kole said.

Sammy fought his way out of Kole's arms, determined to get closer to Cronin. The cat purred and meowed until Cronin grabbed the cat and held it. Alec burst out laughing, Cronin rolled his eyes, and they leapt.

THEY ARRIVED BACK at Cronin's apartment, to find Eiji and Jodis packed, ready and waiting. Kole recoiled from leaping, gasping wide-eyed. "I know leaping hurts," Alec told him, helping him into a coat and fixing the buttons. "You'll get used to it."

Then seven of them, Cronin, Alec, Kole, Jacques, Eiji, Jodis, and Eleanor, picked up all the bags they could carry—including Sammy the cat—and they leapt again.

The house they arrived in this time was light but cold. Not that the vampires seemed to notice, but Alec was grateful for the coat Cronin had told him to get. Jacques took the bags and aligned them against the wall, and Eleanor set about starting the fire.

"Where are we?" Kole asked.

"Japan," Alec told him. He recognized the white walls, dark wood trims, and traditional furniture. The specially filtered glass on the windows allowed sunshine into the house without harming vampires, like the apartment in New York. The view outside, however, was vastly different. Whereas New York was buildings, steel, and glass, this view was all greenery and cherry blossom trees.

Kole looked around the room, then at the view outside. "Japan?" he whispered.

"There was an attack on the New York apartment," Alec explained. "They knew where we were, and they clearly knew where you were too."

"The letter from the museum?" Kole asked.

Eiji and Jodis were now inspecting the letter and tickets Cronin had given them. "The tickets are personalized invitations," Cronin said. "Alec's name is printed on the second ticket."

"The museum has an exhibit of the Terracotta Soldiers," Jodis said quietly. She looked at Alec. "They want you there."

"I didn't think much of it," Kole said. "I joined Alec under my library account when he was a boy, so I just assumed...." He swallowed hard. "This has something to do with Genghis Khan, doesn't it?"

Alec nodded. "Yeah, Dad. It does."

"Surely they'd not be so stupid to assume he would go?" Cronin barked.

"I think I should go," Alec said.

"Alec," Cronin said with a humorless laugh. "Do not think for one second I would allow you to walk into such a trap!"

"You wouldn't *allow* me?" he asked, one eyebrow raised.

Cronin growled in frustration. "You know what I mean, Alec. I cannot bear the thought of you subjecting yourself to this."

"Listen," Alec started. He put his hand on Cronin's arm, the touch calming them both. "I'd prefer to test the waters with five or six of these terracotta soldiers rather than trying my luck with five or six thousand. It makes sense. If not the museum in New York—if you think it's a trap—then surely there are others around the world. London, Sydney, Hong Kong. They've been on exhibit everywhere!"

Eiji nodded. "I agree with Alec." Cronin growled again, but Eiji was undeterred. "Cronin, he's right. It makes sense."

Kole interrupted. "Uh, Alec? What's this about?"

Alec remembered then that his father didn't know the latest discovery. "We believe Genghis Khan has reformed his army. The Terracotta Army has been buried under what was a pyramid, Dad. Jorge said the earth will come to life."

"Earth, as in terracotta?" Kole asked quietly. Alec nodded and Kole looked at the letter Jodis was still holding. "Why did they want me to go?"

Jodis held out the two tickets. "For you to take Alec, it would seem."

Eleanor, who was sitting in front of the now-crackling fire, said, "The tickets are a ruse, yes. I can see that not ending well."

"Thank you!" Cronin cried.

"Surely they can't have been so naïve to assume Alec would actually go to the New York exhibit," Eiji said, shaking his head in disbelief.

"If not Alec," Eleanor said quietly, "then Kole. The deception I see is if not Alec, then Kole as leverage would suffice."

Kole sat himself wearily onto the low sofa. Alec watched as Jacques moved to stand behind his father, realizing Jacques still took his role of protector seriously. Alec smiled at Jacques as he sat beside Kole and clapped him on the back, reassuring him without words.

"Cronin, if you were to go to a different museum," Eleanor suggested. "I foresee no complications. Only answers."

Cronin let his head fall back and he groaned at the ceiling. Alec was quick to stand beside him, to touch him. "I know you don't like it," Alec said softly. "I don't like putting us all at risk either, but the sooner we sort this out the better, yes?"

Cronin gave a petulant snarl, and Alec thought he was particularly cute when he pouted. "Don't smile at me like that, Alec."

"So it's settled," Alec declared. "Would it make you feel better if I let you choose which museum we went to?"

"Let me choose?" Cronin repeated. His lips twisted into a smirk. "You will allow me to make a decision? How very generous."

"Is that sarcasm I detect?" Alec asked with a smile. "I

thought the transfer effects of drinking my blood had started to wear off."

Cronin smiled now. "And let me guess. You want to go to the museum of my choice *right now*."

"Of course."

Cronin sighed, but he pulled Alec in for a hug. He ran his nose along Alec's neck, inhaling deeply. Alec could feel the tension leaving Cronin's body. "Well," Cronin said, "considering my choices are limited to nightfall, you leave me with little choice." He pulled out his phone, pressed some buttons, and put it to his ear. "Kennard, my old friend. What is the security like in the British Museum at 4:00 a.m.?"

BY THE TIME Cronin had made arrangements to meet Kennard inside the British Museum, Eiji had armed himself and Jodis with quivers of arrows and stakes, and Kole had declared he wasn't going anywhere if it involved leaping. Jacques would stay with him, as would Eleanor. Alec knew his father would more than likely go back to bed, considering it was after midnight, New York time.

In truth, Alec realized, his dad looked like he could use the rest. He looked tired, worn, and worried. "Be safe, huh?" was all Kole said before Alec, Cronin, Eiji, and Jodis disappeared.

In what was his third country in less than an hour, Alec found himself standing inside the British Museum. It was lit only by security lighting, the room was huge with high glass ceilings. Everything else was marble and tile, including the stairs that wrapped around both sides of the round room. They'd landed in the Great Court, and Kennard along with two vampires Alec had not met before, greeted them with warm smiles.

Cronin greeted them with a blunt, "Security?"

Kennard waved his hand toward the far wall, where Alec assumed there were offices. "Taken care of," he said smugly. "Davis here ensured the video surveillance will play on a loop of empty rooms, and Julia helped the guards to sleep. They'll wake up just fine after we've gone, of course."

Alec hated to admit that as a cop he'd detest what they were doing, but now he was on the other side of the ethical fence, he thought their ability to remain undetected was pretty damn cool.

The tall male vampire, who Alec assumed to be Davis, bowed his head to Alec. "It is an honor," he said, his British accent thick.

The woman, Julia, followed suit. "And a privilege," she said, sounding more Cockney.

Alec swallowed hard. He would never get used to people treating him as though he were royalty or something. "Um, thanks?"

Eiji laughed and shook hands with Kennard. "It's been too long, my friend."

Kennard grinned widely. "You're feeling better?"

"Much."

Then Kennard took Jodis' hand, and Alec half expected him to kiss it. He didn't, though, he slightly bowed instead. "My memory does your beauty injustice."

Jodis rolled her eyes. "Yet I remember your *charms* just fine."

Kennard laughed and Jodis smiled at him. It was clear they were old friends, and Alec envied their history. He was such a newcomer, so young compared to them all, and it was mind-blowing to think Alec's entire lifespan of twenty-nine years must have felt like a week to them.

"Alec," Kennard cooed. He smoothly took Alec's hand and looked up at him.

Cronin growled, making Kennard laugh. "I see someone has his jealous pants on today."

Cronin's growl got louder and a lot more serious, and Kennard stopped smiling. He turned to Cronin and raised an eyebrow in question.

Eiji quickly stood between them and pulled Kennard's hand from Alec's. "He means nothing of it. It seems there are undue consequences from drinking Alec's blood."

Alec quickly stepped around Eiji so he could touch Cronin. He put one arm around him, standing half side-on to Kennard.

Jodis added. "Or from being fated to a human, we don't know. There are many questions and very few answers."

Kennard blinked, his expression grew concerned. "Why did you not say anything?"

"Changes in Cronin's behavior are not something we want made public," Alec said.

"Hmm," Kennard hummed with a serious nod. "A point I can understand."

"I apologize," Cronin said quietly. "I cannot help it, or so it seems."

"My friend," Kennard said warmly. "Apologies not required. I was unaware. But rest assured, I won't touch him." Then he smiled. "Unless he wants me to."

Cronin growled again.

Kennard's lips twisted. "Or make jokes about it either, apparently."

Alec tightened his arm around Cronin, wanting—no, not wanting, *needing*—to reassure him. To protect him, to ground him and soothe him. And in that moment, Alec knew if Kennard or anyone else tried to touch Cronin, he'd do more than growl at them himself.

"It seems it's a mutual symbiosis," Kennard mused, looking at how Alec was almost curling around Cronin.

Jodis nodded. "We need to fight whatever war is coming and finish it before this symbiosis"—she nodded toward Alec and Cronin—"as you call it, becomes irreparable."

This time Alec growled and Cronin's hold on him tightened. "We're not broken," he murmured.

Kennard eyed them both cautiously with a look on his face that clearly said, *Well, you're not too freakin' normal either,* but he very wisely changed subject. "Tell me what you've uncovered since we visited Jorge."

As they told him what they'd learned and of the attack in New York, Alec looked around the museum. Alec could see it was grand, even in the dark. To the left, guarding an entrance to what was obviously the Egyptian exhibit, were two statues. Memories of Egyptian mummies—the screams they made and the unholy stench of death—assaulted Alec's mind, and he shivered from head to foot.

Cronin noticed, of course, and looked to see what had caught Alec's eye. But then Alec had noticed something else. To the right of the cylindrical room were two large banners, both easily twelve feet tall, each picture was of a Terracotta Soldier standing guard at the door.

Not paying any attention to what the others were saying, Alec was drawn to the right. Whether it was fate or curiosity, Alec found himself walking toward the Ancient Chinese exhibition.

When he got to the door, he stopped. "Alec," Cronin said. He was right behind him, and Alec was of the impression it was not the first time Cronin had called his name—

he'd just not heard it. He was so engrossed, so hypnotized by the lure of the Terracotta Army. All seven vampires were now behind him, watching him cautiously. Eiji and Jodis both now had wooden stakes in their hands.

"This way," Alec said quietly. It was almost dreamlike, like he was almost floating, but he led them into the room.

There were square pillars lining the long and narrow room, holding up the grand and ornate ceiling. Alongside the pillars were glass cabinets of antiques that normally Alec would love to inspect and question, but in that moment he cared for none of it. Because in the center of the room, behind glass walls, were six Terracotta Soldiers. They faced him, stoic and still, like they were waiting just for him.

Four foot soldiers stood and two archers knelt in combat formation, and Alec stood before them. The silence was deafening, everything was eerily still, though it was far from peaceful. Alec's heart was hammering, his gut instinct was telling him to turn and run, yet he stood as motionless as the terracotta men before him.

Then a strangled, horrific bray broke the silence like thunder. Alec spun to the sound to see a lone terracotta cavalryman tethered to a terracotta horse in a glass room. The horse, with its mouth open and its eyes wide, pulled its head back, braying again. Slowly it lifted one foot, and when it stomped to the ground, the terracotta foot broke off and the animal screamed.

Then in an unfolding horror, the six terracotta men in front of him moved. The foot soldiers moved their arms, as if lifting weapons they weren't holding, and the kneeling archers slowly stood up and aimed their arrows at Alec.

CHAPTER TEN

ALEC STUMBLED BACKWARDS and Cronin quickly caught him. Eiji and Jodis moved in front of him, each with stakes in both hands, and never taking their eyes off the threat, they walked backwards, slowly out of the room. Alec saw one of the foot soldiers take one step before they rounded the corner.

Cronin yelled, "Take a hold!"

Everyone held out their hands, touching, and Cronin leapt. Suddenly, Alec found himself in a dark alley, and not just any alley, but the one behind Kennard's club in London. Alec watched as the seven vampires enclosed around him, keenly scanning their surroundings, before Cronin pulled Alec against him.

It was Kennard who laughed. "Well that was entertaining!" he said. His eyes were alight and his smile wide, making his boyish features look more impish than vampire. "Alec, you are a treasure. First it was mummies. Now statues come to life before you."

"If you three are well, we'll be on our way," Cronin said tightly.

"Yes, of course," Kennard said. Both Davis and Julia nodded, but kept their eyes on Alec, wide with wonder. "Do keep me informed," Kennard continued. "And remember, if you need numbers in China, just let me know."

Eiji bowed in return, and no sooner had he touched Jodis, than Cronin reached out his hand and they were gone again.

As soon as Alec's feet hit solid ground, he saw the familiar living room of the house in Japan and he sighed. Eleanor stood waiting, expectant. "I saw what happened," she said. "Only a moment before it did. I had no way to warn you. I knew there would be answers, but I was not expecting them to be so rash."

"Answers?" Cronin snapped. "To what? All we have now is more questions."

Alec ignored their bickering. "Where is my father?"

"He sleeps, and Jacques stands guard," Eleanor answered. "Alec, I am sorry for not forewarning you. I feel my gift around you lessens with time. The gap between the vision and the actual occurrence is decreasing. Either they have a cloaker or your blood affects what I see. I simply do not know."

Cronin sighed, yet his hold on Alec tightened. He looked at Eleanor. "Apologies for my ill-temper. It seems the effects Alec has on talents is wide spreading."

Eleanor bowed her head to her elder. "Your apology is humbly accepted, though your concern is warranted. Fear not to offend. We will overcome these troubled times, Cronin."

Alec's head began to swim with all the leaping and the events of the night. "I've had just about all the excitement I care for today. Watching stone statues come to life in front of me is right up alongside mummies on my I-never-want-to-see-again list."

Cronin's brow furrowed. "Alec, are you well?"

Alec leaned into him, craving his warmth and strength, wrapped both arms around him as tight as he dared, and he sighed deeply. He didn't need to reply with words, but Cronin responded in kind. Jodis cleared her throat. "We will start researching masonry effects and influences," she said. "Join us once Alec is sleeping."

Cronin gave a nod in answer, and without a word, took Alec's hand and led him out of the room. Alec assumed Cronin somehow knew he'd had enough leaping for one day, because they walked. The bedroom at the end of the long hall was dark and Alec could barely make out the bed. It was a low-set futon-style bed that looked invitingly soft. He stripped out of his clothes, despite how cool the room was, and lay down face-first on the mattress.

Not a second later, Cronin crawled up his body, planting kisses on the back of his calves, his thighs, his ass, his spine, and finally the back of his neck. "Alec, you are cold."

Alec smiled and lifted his ass in invitation. "Then stop talking and warm me up."

Eiji called out from down the hall. "This house has thin walls."

Alec muffled his laugh with a pillow. "Then you can thank me later."

Cronin scraped his fangs across the back of Alec's neck before kissing the exposed skin. Alec pushed his forehead into the pillow, craning his neck to give Cronin more skin, groaning without shame.

Alec found himself being turned over, cradled in Cronin's talented and tentative hands. He was on his back in less time than it took to blink. Cronin was above him, naked and demanding, his eyes were pools of dark desire, and he ran his tongue along his fangs. Alec moaned with want, and Cronin kissed him quiet, covering Alec's mouth with his own.

Their cocks aligned as Cronin thrust and ground against him. Alec spread his thighs wider and tilted his hips, wanting everything Cronin had. He ran his hands down Cronin's back and over the swell of his ass, pulling their hips together, seeking friction where he wanted it most. Their cocks slid against their bodies, slicked with precome and need, their mouths were fused, and tongues tangled and tasted.

Alec had never craved anything like this. He needed Cronin with every cell in his body. It wasn't enough. It would never be enough. Never touch enough, never taste enough. They would never be close enough. And with gripping hands and desperate moans, a pleasure so divine, so complete, detonated in Alec's belly. Like nuclear fallout, it unfurled in slow motion and light speed at the same time, blinding and consuming.

With his head thrown back, his mouth opened in a silent scream, his neck corded, and his whole body taut and convulsing, Alec came.

Cronin held onto him, bucking against him, and with a growl in Alec's ear, he spilled between them.

Alec wrapped his arms around him as Cronin collapsed on top of him. Alec loved the weight of his body pressing down on him, and he tightened his hold. Cronin was purring and mumbling nonsensical things Alec couldn't make out. He kissed the side of Cronin's head, and just before he fell asleep, he whispered something Cronin had once said to him. *"Rug mi ort, m'cridhe."*

I have you, my heart.

ALEC WOKE up not knowing where he was. It was a strange bed in a strange room, and Alec remembered then. They were in Japan. There was light, and Alec had been so used to Cronin's bedroom in the New York apartment where the bedroom window had been blacked out.

Mmm, Cronin.

Alec stretched out in bed, feeling contentment in every inch of his body. He also felt something else stirring in his balls and gave his morning wood a squeeze.

"Oh Alec, for the love of Freya," Jodis complained from the living room. "Cronin take him and his human pheromones away."

Alec snorted out a laugh and rolled out of bed. He took a piss, showered, threw on some jeans, and walked, shirtless, out into the living room. They were all seated on the sofas with books and laptops, and Alec's whiteboard was now against one wall. The once-tranquil Japanese room now looked like an operational combat headquarters.

Without acknowledging anyone else in the room, Alec walked straight over to Cronin and dropped onto the sofa beside him. He maneuvered Cronin's arm so he fit snugly against him and wriggled himself in nice and warm. Cronin pushed the old textbook away so he could wrap both arms around Alec.

"Morning," Alec said, his voice still thick from sleep.

Eiji laughed. "Make yourself comfortable. Don't let our presence stop you."

"I won't," Alec said with a smile.

Cronin kissed the side of his head. "You slept well?"

"Mm," Alec hummed. "Woke up alone though."

Cronin nuzzled into Alec's hair. "Apologies."

Alec squirmed against him and Cronin started to purr in his ear. Jodis whined. "Please, you two."

Alec laughed and squirmed some more. "I can't help it. He's so damn good at what he does to me—" His words cut off in his throat when he saw Kole walk in from the kitchen. Alec sat up. "Dad! I forgot you were here!"

Eiji laughed. "Ah, metaphorical cold water."

Alec gave Eiji the stink eye as he stood up and walked over to his father. Kole was holding a plate of toast, and Alec helped himself to a slice. He bit into it, and Kole put his hand to Alec's chin and turned his head to the side. He frowned.

"What?" Alec said with his mouth half-full.

Kole shrugged and shook his head. "Nothing."

But then Alec remembered. He had bite marks—literal vampire bite marks up his neck. They were only small, purplish puncture wounds, but he instantly regretted forgoing the shirt. He wasn't ashamed—hell, the very opposite was true —but sometimes there were things a father shouldn't have to see. He swallowed his food, and although his hand automatically went to cover the bite marks, he stopped himself. Instead, he raised his chin and looked his father in the eye.

"It's one thing to know it. I guess it's just different to see it," Kole said quietly.

Alec nodded. "It's who I am, Dad. It's who Cronin is, and it's who I will be."

Kole studied Alec for a long moment. If he was looking for doubt or fear in Alec's eyes, then he found none. He never would. Eventually he nodded. "You could at least put some clothes on," Kole said. "There are ladies in the room."

"How will everyone appreciate my awesome body if I cover it up?" Alec asked with a roll of his eyes, and when he turned to go and get a freakin' shirt, Cronin stood behind him with a neatly folded shirt in his hands.

He was fighting a smile. "I will make you coffee."

Alec pulled the button down shirt over his head and ignored the fact that Eiji was grinning from ear to ear. He deliberately looked at Jodis. "So, you guys have been busy." He nodded toward the books and whiteboard.

"We went back for them while you slept," she explained. "Well, Cronin and I went back, Eiji, Jacques, and Eleanor stayed here."

"Had anyone else been in the apartment?" Alec asked.

Jodis shook her head. "It didn't appear so. There were no scents of any others."

Cronin sat down beside Alec and handed him his coffee. "We were only gone for half a minute."

"I didn't feel it," Alec murmured.

"You were sleeping deeply," Cronin replied.

"Cronin didn't fare so well," Jodis said. "Even half a minute of your absence clawed at him."

Alec leaned into him, almost subconsciously, and pressed his lips to Cronin's shoulder in a silent apology for not being there. "You guys have been busy, though. What have we learned?"

"We can't find any reference to stone reacting to a human," Jodis said.

"Didn't you say there were masons, people who control stone?" Alec sipped his coffee.

"*Vampires* who can control stone," Eiji corrected. "Not humans, except you. Anyway, you didn't control those statues. They reacted to your presence."

"Which is also unprecedented," Cronin said quietly. "As far as we can tell."

"It has to be something to do with my blood, right?" Alec asked. He looked out the window to see it was getting dark, then glanced at his watch. "I've crossed so many time zones in the last twenty-four hours, I don't even know what day it is anymore. I need to call Doctor Benavides."

Cronin didn't even have to look at anything. Like he had a world clock in his head, he said, "It is almost 6:00 p.m. here, almost 4:00 a.m. in New York."

"So I can call in a few hours?" Alec asked. So much had happened since he'd had blood taken, it felt like a week not barely two days. Then he remembered something. "Eiji, you said you couldn't see my ancestors. Have you read my Dad yet? Maybe he can show you something more?"

Eiji gave a nod. "Yes, when he awoke earlier, with the same results. I can see three generations back, then something blurs out. It is the same as yours. From what I can see"—he put his hand up and drew a vertical line in the air which Alec deduced was how he saw DNA in his head—"it goes straight, then on your paternal great-great grandmother's side, it blurs." He opened his hand as though the DNA in his mind's eye vanished into nothing.

Alec didn't know what to make of it. "My great-great grandmother?"

"Yes. My great grandmother," Kole added with a shrug. "I never knew her. She died in childbirth having my grandfather, or so the family tree says. It wasn't too uncommon back in those days."

Alec shook his head vehemently and put his half-finished coffee on the side table. "It can't be a coincidence." He thought about what it all could mean and looked at Cronin. "Tell me, how does the whole incubus thing work?"

Cronin blinked in surprise, and when Alec looked at the others, he found all the vampires staring at him. "Incubus?"

"Well, it would explain a few things, yes?" Alec pressed on. "What if my great-great grandmother was impregnated by a vampire? The birth killed her, and the baby is born human but with special blood."

"I don't know," Jodis started to say, as though it was too farfetched a notion.

Alec shook his head, even more convinced he was right. "You know, I've seen mummified vampires come back to life, I've seen terracotta statues move, and let's not forget the terracotta horse that screamed, right? Because for me, that's right up there with the evil sounds and horrid smell of rancid mummies on my will-have-nightmares-about-that-shit list. So really, the possibility that I'm a direct descendant of a vampire is probably the least-weirdest shit that's happened to me."

Cronin took Alec's hand and squeezed it. "Alec, in theory, it is feasible."

"But?"

"The child conceived by an incubus, if it survives gestation, is born a vampire," Cronin said quietly. "Your grandfathers were not."

"What if it was genetically redundant until me?" Alec asked. "What if the genes had to wait until my parents were the right genetic combination?" Then he stopped, because something else crept into his consciousness. A thought—no, a realization—that made his blood run cold.

"Alec, what is it?" Cronin asked, concerned.

"My mother," he whispered. He looked at Kole. "Her death wasn't random. Those two vampires, who were in my room when I was newborn, weren't there to kill me, or take me, or whatever we assumed they were there for. They were there to kill my mother. She's the missing link."

Kole shook his head. His face was pale. "Alec, what are you saying?"

"Our blood is special," Alec said, his voice gathered momentum. "We've always known that. It's what we were told by your grandfather and his father, yes?"

Kole nodded.

"And if it is because we're descendants of an incubus, we have vampire blood, but we're human. What if my mother was the same? What if her bloodline was the same, a descendant of vampire? As a single bloodline, it's nothing too extraordinary: we heal fast, we think fast, we have a photographic memory, but when two vampire bloodlines cross," Alec said with a smile. He knew he was right. He'd never been so sure. "What we have, is a—"

"Human key," Cronin finished.

Alec nodded. "Yes. When two vampire bloodlines cross, we have exactly that. We have me."

CHAPTER ELEVEN

ALEC USED every avenue he could think of, short of hacking into the NYPD computer system, to trace his mother's family tree. Not that criminal histories would be much use from police records, but after genealogy sites came up empty, he needed to search outside the box.

All the while Eiji kept his hand on Alec's arm—much to the disdain of Cronin—to see if he could channel into his maternal readings.

He found nothing past the third generation. It was as though his genetic slate had been wiped clean. He found nothing.

Alec had read and reread the family tree book Cronin had asked Kole to bring with him, and there in his mother's cursive handwriting, were the names of his mother, her mother, and her mother. Then nothing.

And those names brought up nothing.

"They were Scottish born," Alec said, thinking aloud. "Can we try old church records of the area, or census data?" He quickly typed in a search for census dates in Scotland.

"There was a census in 1901. If we cross reference names—"

His words were cut off when his father, obviously upset, walked out of the room. With a heavy sigh, Alec pushed the laptop away and followed him. He found him in the small kitchenette starting to fix himself a pot of tea. "Dad?"

Kole left the teapot and shook his head. "I know it might explain something, Alec. But to what end? It doesn't change anything."

"Because then I'll know," Alec said. "Something isn't right in my makeup, Dad. Something that makes my blood special, something that affects Cronin. Doesn't that bother you?"

Kole faced his son. "Of course it does. But it doesn't bring her back."

"No, it doesn't," Alec said quietly. "But it could save my life. Or Cronin's. And that's something I can't *not* do, Dad. If it could save Cronin, then I *have* to."

Alec looked up to find Cronin standing in the doorway. He walked in slowly, giving Alec a small smile. "Your father is right," Cronin said, taking Alec's hand. "It changes nothing. Alec, I think your theory on joined vampire bloodlines has credence. It's absurd and fantastical, but no more so than anything else we've encountered. It does explain a lot, and as much as we try to search for answers, there will be none. There's never been a human key before, so to unearth memories of your mother will only serve to upset your father."

Alec sighed again and looked to the floor. "Okay. I know. Sorry, Dad."

Kole gave him a sad smile. "'S'okay Alec. But thank you, Cronin."

"Here!" Eiji said, suddenly appearing in the kitchen

with an old, old book open in his hand. "In the ninth century, there was a record of a small child in Jakarta who had no past line or future line when touched by a reader—" Eiji paused, and looked to Alec and Kole to explain. "—like me. I am called a reader. This child had no past, no future. His mother claimed to have been seduced and impregnated by an incubus!"

"His mother lived?" Cronin asked.

"Well," Eiji made a face, "she survived the birth, yes. But they killed them both right then. They didn't like the unknown apparently, but it was documented."

"So you think my theory of my blood being descended of vampires could be correct?" Alec asked him.

Eiji shrugged and his smile became a grin. "I do."

"It doesn't explain why your mother was killed though," Cronin said quietly.

"Maybe she knew. Maybe she was in on it somehow," Alec offered. He looked at his father and tamped down any excitement. "But it doesn't matter. It's not important now if she knew or not. Dad's right; it won't bring her back."

Frowning, Kole shook his head. "If she knew anything, she never said."

Alec sighed and let his head fall back. "Well, I need to research what will give me answers. Eleanor mentioned five segments in a stone that Genghis had. I need to figure out what the hell that is."

"Uh, maybe I could help with that," Jacques said. "I studied world histories at university."

"University?" Alec asked. He didn't know vampires went to college.

Jacques smiled at him. "When I was human, I attended la Sorbonne in the 1920s." He seemed to blush a little. "I am skilled at tactical defense, yes. That's why I was asked to watch over Kole, but world histories are my passion."

Alec grinned back at the French vampire. "Eleanor," Alec said, knowing wherever she was in the house, she would hear. "Can you please explain to Jacques what you saw about the stone plate?"

While everyone else stood around the living room, Eleanor sat on the sofa, and used her hands to describe the stone plate she'd seen in her vision. "A large dinner-plate-sized stone disc, two inches thick," she said. "It's quartered into four segments, but there's a circle in the center, which is the fifth section. It's in a room that's well guarded. Whatever it is, it's important to him."

Jacques nodded. "Yes, there are four mythological symbols of China," he said. "They each represent an element. The azure dragon is wood, the white tiger is metal, the black tortoise is water, and the vermilion bird is fire."

"But this has five sections," Alec reminded him.

Jacques nodded toward the whiteboard. "May I?"

"Please."

On the board, Jacques drew a circle and quartered it, quickly writing in each of the four symbols. Within the circle he drew a center circle, much like a bull's-eye on a dartboard, and pointed to it. "This central element touches all symbols. It is the most powerful. Each symbol also represents the seasons, of which we know there are only four. Given that, over the last centuries in Chinese culture, there has been much debate over the fifth symbol and some claim it does not exist."

The room was deathly quiet. All eyes were on Jacques. Jodis spoke first. "What's the fifth symbol?"

Alec knew without a doubt what the fifth symbol was. He just *knew*. He answered. "Stone."

Jacques nodded. "Yes. Stone or earth. Central, touching all other elements, garnering all powers."

Eiji nodded, looking at Cronin. "It would explain why you could transfer all powers from those around you after you drank Alec's blood," Eiji said. "And why our powers could conduct through him."

Cronin started to growl. His jaw set hard and his black eyes glinted. "I don't like it. There are too many forces at play here. There is too much we cannot control."

Alec slid his hands around Cronin's neck and pulled him against him. "But answers are good. I don't mind, as long as we know what we're up against. And as long as we go into this together. We'll be okay."

"Eleanor," Jodis asked. "Has anything changed?"

The old woman vampire sat still for a moment then swayed her head. Her milky eyes moved and flickered, seeing things that only she could see. "No changes. Alec will still be unwell. Whatever happens there affects only him. It is very difficult to see." She made a pained face. "There's a cloaker trying to hide it from me. I'm sure of it."

Cronin growled a little louder and pulled back and turned from Alec. "Eiji, you and I could leap there right now and take them out."

Alec grabbed Cronin's shirt and pulled him back around, suddenly very angry. "Hey. Together, remember? As in partners. What's to say they don't have a seer just like Eleanor, and they know you're coming? They could give you both a little welcoming party with a stake to the fucking heart."

Cronin blinked, clearly taken aback by Alec's tone. "I was—"

Alec's grip tightened on Cronin's shirt and he growled. "Well you can just fucking stop it. We go together. Always."

Cronin pressed himself against Alec, growling a deep rumbling sound. His eyes drilled into Alec's. His fangs gleamed at the corners of his mouth. Alec felt instant desire pool in his belly.

"Ugh," Eiji groaned. "Please, you two. Enough with the sexual tension!"

"Take it somewhere else," Eleanor chimed in, ruffling her shirt collar as though she was suddenly hot.

Alec smiled despite his thrumming blood. He gnashed his very human teeth and pretended to bite Cronin's neck. Alec heard Eleanor say, "One hour, Cronin," and suddenly he found himself on his back in a strange bed.

Cronin knelt over him, all domineering and growling. "Don't ever bite a vampire on the neck," Cronin said, his voice low and gruff.

Alec grinned and threw Cronin off, pinning him down for a change. Cronin seemed surprised by Alec's burst of strength. His dark eyes went wide, and his growl ripped through the air.

Alec held Cronin's arms to the bed, their faces barely an inch apart. "Where are we?"

"Penthouse suite, Armani Milano," Cronin answered in a purr. "It's vacant and locked."

"You sound like you've done this before," Alec whispered, his lips touching Cronin's.

Smiling, Cronin rocked his hips. "You know I've done no such thing."

Alec ground against him, hard, spreading Cronin's thighs wider. He'd never felt so powerful, so dominant and possessive. "You don't talk about going anywhere with anyone else," Alec growled at him and let go of one of Cronin's arms so he could turn his head, exposing Cronin's neck. "And if I want to bite your neck, I fucking will."

And he did. He sunk his teeth into Cronin's neck, and Cronin arched underneath him, flexing as he came. Fully clothed and his cock untouched, Cronin convulsed as his orgasm took hold. All Alec could do was hold on and watch, in rapt awe, as Cronin unraveled underneath him.

He eventually calmed, seemingly boneless and pliant. He looked drunk and smiley, his fangs peeking out under his pink, pink lips. His eyes half-opened and he smirked. "*A Chruthaidheir,*" he mumbled. "*Gràidhean.*"

Alec put his hands to Cronin's face, kissing him soundly. "In English?"

Cronin laughed and his eyes rolled back. "Oh God, my love."

Alec kissed him with smiling lips. "Teach me Gaelic words for you."

Cronin gripped Alec's face, staring deeply into his eyes. "*Mo ghaol bith-buan,*" he whispered, so reverently, the words sounded like a prayer.

Alec waited for him to translate.

"My eternal love."

Alec repeated the words. "Mo ghaol bith-buan."

Cronin swallowed hard and his eyes were molten onyx. He stared at Alec, taking in his whole face before bringing their mouths together. This time they made love, with slow breaths and tender thrusts, holding hands and kissing softly, they never, ever, closed their eyes.

Alec had never felt so full and content. Cronin was inside him, yes, but in more ways than one. He permeated every sense, every cell, and from the way Cronin held him, filled him, it was like he was trying to become one with him.

Alec had learned some words in Gaelic from his time with Cronin, but some things needed to be said in English. He took Cronin's face in his hands, taking in his lust-black eyes, his kiss-swollen lips, and his vampire fangs. "I love you, too."

WITH ONLY SECONDS TO SPARE, an hour after they left, Cronin and Alec leapt back to the house in Japan. Still wrapped around each other, Alec was biting his bottom lip and Cronin was chuckling.

"Ugh, stop it!" Eiji cried with a groan. Cronin laughed, not because Eiji was begging, but because he said it in Japanese. It wasn't often he spoke in his native tongue.

"I can't help it," Alec said, half laughing against Cronin's head. He clearly didn't need Cronin to interpret what Eiji had said. His groan and desperate tone must have said it all.

"You're getting worse," Jodis said.

"At least we're dressed," Alec said, making Cronin laugh. "Though the cleaning staff of that hotel will be little perplexed."

Eiji snorted out a laugh, despite grumbling just before. "You two *are* getting worse," he repeated what Jodis said. "The hormonal scents coming from you two are suffocating, and it's worse now than what it's ever been. Can you at least be in the same room without touching?"

Alec made a low growling noise and tightened his grip on Cronin, which was a very clear nonverbal no. "What did we have to be back for in an hour anyway?" he asked. "We could have stayed a lot longer."

No sooner had he said it than Alec's cell phone rang. "Because that's why," Eleanor said.

With one arm still around Cronin, Alec read the screen.

"It's Doctor Benavides," he announced and then hit the answer button. "Hi Doc, you're on speaker."

"Alec, yes. I have your results," the doctor said.

"Good. What did you find? Traces of Kryptonite?"

"Not quite," the doctor said. It sounded like he was smiling. "White cell counts were normal, platelet count was great. Red cell counts were... unusual. Your corpuscular hemoglobin concentration was low, which at first glance I thought was wrong."

"Why?"

"It's a blood result typical of burn patients, which you're clearly not," the doctor said. "The hemoglobin is very concentrated within the red cell. With you, even more so. I thought it was a misreading, but then there were more results that didn't add up."

Alec frowned. "And?"

"Well, I ran a string of tests, just like you asked. And that included a serum protein electrophoresis test. Now, you've always had high iron," Doctor Benavides said. "And you still do. But these readings are... well, very unusual."

"Describe unusual."

"Well, the proteins in your blood are all over the place, Alec. And the readings don't make sense." There was the sound of rustling papers. "Your adenosine triphosphate is elevated. As is your adrenocorticotropic hormone, and your transferrin levels are off the charts."

Alec frowned and his eyebrows furrowed. "What does that mean, Doc? I'm gonna need that in English."

"In a very simplified analogy, Alec, adenosine triphosphate is basically energy, and adrenocorticotropic hormones fire up the cerebral cortex. Transferrin is a blood protein that binds iron to blood cells. Too much of it can cause hemochromatosis in humans, but Alec, you've got no other readings to imply too much iron. And from your blood tests last year, these results are new. It doesn't make sense."

Cronin could feel Jodis and Eiji's eyes upon him. The doctor was wrong: it was starting to make perfect sense.

"What do I have to do?" Alec asked.

"Well, I can run all the tests again," Doctor Benavides said. "Though I'm not sure it'll make any difference. Alec, I'm going to be frank with you. With these readings, I'd say you'd need hospitalization and further tests for liver function, cardiomyopathy, bone density, and brain function. It's not good, Alec."

Alec had become pale, and he looked at Cronin, then to Jodis and Eiji, and finally back to Cronin. His voice was quiet and distant. "'S'okay, Doc. I don't think I'll need to worry about that."

"Alec, I don't—"

"Doc, it's fine," Alec replied. He looked again at Jodis and Eiji. "Thank you for doing this. Something tells me these readings aren't as big a surprise as you'd think."

He clicked off the call and slid the phone across the table, away from him. He stared straight at Cronin. "Tell me what that means. I can tell from the look on your faces you know something."

Cronin took Alec's hand and led him to sit down on the sofa. "I don't know anything scientific, Alec," Cronin said. "Though what the doctor found makes perfect sense. These elevated blood compounds are a seamless explanation of the power in your blood."

"How?" Alec asked. "Because all I heard was liver, heart, and brain complications."

Cronin shook his head quickly. "No, Alec. It will never get to that. I swear it to you."

Jodis sat on the other side of Alec. She took his other

hand and shook her head. "Cronin's right, Alec. The three elevated elements, or compounds, in your blood results are the three main fuel source for vampires," she explained. "Pure proteins of energy, pure cerebral cortex power, and iron for oxygenation and brain function and muscle power."

"It's like high-octane fuel," Eiji added. "One-hundred-percent battery power."

Alec bit his bottom lip and seemed lost in his own thoughts for a while. "Is that what Jorge meant about the sun in my blood? Maybe he wasn't talking about sunlight beaming out of the sun-disk thing in Egypt. Maybe he literally meant the power of the sun, as in energy."

"Possibly," Cronin answered. "It certainly explains how it healed Eiji so quickly."

"And why Cronin's experiencing high levels of... well, everything," Jodis said. She looked straight at Cronin. "You can transfer talents, you can't be apart from him, higher needs of dependency, you're more in tune with each other than most fated couples of a thousand years. Everything is intensified."

"And it all but confirms the theory of Alec's blood being descendent from vampires," Eiji furthered. "If the incubus who impregnated his great-grandmother had just fed, then it stands to reason those three elements would be high in his blood, and genetically transferred down through the generations."

"And it's killing me," Alec said quietly. "Even Eleanor said my blood's too powerful for a human to survive." He gave Cronin a tight smile and shrugged. "If we don't fight this war soon, or whatever it is we're supposed to do, then I won't be in any condition to fight at all. You guys are seemingly forgetting one thing: I'm human. Mortal. Unlike you, my system will shut down with a no-restart option. And if I can't be changed into a vampire, then it really is game over."

Cronin growled, a low rumbling sound, coming from deep in his belly. As though growling was all he was capable of—like he couldn't fathom such an idea, he couldn't even grasp the words to say. His vocabulary, his voice, failed him.

Alec understood that completely. He swallowed hard. "I'm just gonna grab some air," he said, standing up and walking toward the front door. He didn't wait for anyone to say anything. He simply walked down the steps into the entrance foyer and out to where no vampire could follow.

Into the sunlight.

CHAPTER TWELVE

CRONIN PACED. He hated feeling so helpless, so far away. Alec was barely a few feet from him, but standing in the sunlight—where Cronin simply could not go—it may as well have been miles between them.

He knew Alec needed some time to get his head around everything, and Cronin had no problem with that. He had a problem with not being able to get to him if he needed to. Cronin paced some more.

Kole, who must have woken at some point, clapped his hand on Cronin's shoulder as he walked past, walking straight outside to his son. "You okay?" Kole asked him.

Alec acknowledged his dad with a small smile, but left his question unanswered. Which, to Cronin, was an answer in itself. No, he was not okay.

"The doctor called," Alec said. And as Alec then proceeded to tell him what Doctor Benavides had said, Eiji put his hand on Cronin's arm.

"He'll be okay," Eiji whispered so no human could hear him. "Cronin, my brother, I will vow my life upon it."

"He's getting stronger," Cronin said just as quietly.

"Physically. He was able to flip me over, something he certainly hasn't been capable of before."

Eiji's eyes widened. "He was stronger than you?"

Cronin gave a slight nod. "Momentarily, yes. He's changing, Eiji. Even his doctor said as much. Those blood results are new."

"You think since he was fated to you, he changed physically as well?"

"It is a possibility I can't ignore," Cronin said. He watched Alec as he talked with his father in the sunshine. "Or, maybe my biting him did change him, just not as we would expect. Or maybe it is our... coupling." Cronin cringed at discussing such personal matters.

Eiji almost smiled. "They could all be possibilities. Maybe it's a combination of all three. We have no way of knowing. We can't change anything from your being fated. That is done. You've stopped biting him, yes?"

Cronin nodded.

"Then your only other way to determine your theory is to stop taking him to bed," Eiji said.

Alec spun around and watched them through the door.

"Did he just hear me?" Eiji spoke in a whisper again, something no human should be able to hear.

"Of course I can hear you," Alec answered. "I may be a mere human, but I'm not deaf."

Eiji and Cronin stared at Alec. "Alec," Cronin said cautiously. "Can I ask that you please come inside?"

Alec rolled his eyes and smiled as he walked in. "Only because you asked so politely." When he saw the looks on their faces, his smile died. "What's wrong?"

Eiji spoke again, the gentlest of murmurs only vampires can hear. To the human ear, it was no more than a breeze.

"Alec, only well-endowed men can hear me speaking right now."

Alec blanched, his wide eyes darting between Eiji and Cronin. But then he barked out a laugh. "What the hell? What drugs are you on?"

"What?" Kole asked, clearly having no clue what was going on.

Jodis and Jacques appeared in the foyer, evidently having heard the whole conversation. "Ah, Alec," Cronin said, using a normal voice so Kole could hear. "You shouldn't have been able to hear us just now."

"Well, if you wanna talk shit about me, it might help if you don't do it four feet from me."

Cronin smiled at him and spoke in a hushed breath, a vampire whisper. "You seem to have acquired the hearing capabilities of a vampire."

Alec looked at all the faces looking at him, seeing how concerned they were. He turned to his father. "Did you hear what Cronin just said?"

Kole frowned back at him. "He didn't speak, son. You feeling okay?"

"Yes, he did," Alec mumbled, turning back to Cronin. "You did, right? I'm not losing my freakin' mind?"

Cronin took Alec's hand. "Yes, I did. Vampires have exceptional hearing. We can have conversations not privy to the human ear. But *you*, a human, heard us talking."

Alec nodded. "I did."

Jodis, standing some eight feet away, with her wide blue eyes swimming with concern, whispered, "Can you hear me?"

"Yes," Alec said. "Of course I can hear you."

Cronin gestured to outside. "The birds? Traffic?"

Alec turned toward the sunshine and tilted his head.

He hadn't noticed before, but now that he concentrated....
He looked back to Cronin and nodded.

"Okay, this changes things," Eiji said, pulling Alec into
the living room. Cronin was quick to be between them,
growling and forcibly removing Eiji's hand from Alec's arm.

When he realized what he'd done, Cronin shook his
head and put up both his hands. "Apologies. I do not mean
what I do."

Eiji nodded slowly, and he eyed them cautiously. Jodis
was behind her mate, defensively, protectively, and the air
in the room was tense. "Whatever it is that affects you both
is getting worse," Jodis said. "We need to put a stop to it."

Cronin spoke quietly to Eiji, his head bowed. "I know
you would never harm him. I am losing control over this."
He swallowed hard. His bond to Alec was so strong, Cronin
knew Alec would feel his distress. Yet he seemed unable to
stop it. "I fear this connection is so overwhelming it's
sending me mad."

Alec put his arms around Cronin and pulled him
against him, burying Cronin's face into the crook of his
neck. He kissed the side of his head and shook his head.
"You're not mad. This is new to everyone. There's never
been a vampire fated to a human before, let alone a human
key. So this is unchartered territory, that's all. You're not
going mad, my love." Alec kissed Cronin's temple again,
before cupping his face so he could look into his eyes. He
spoke fiercely. "You're not going mad."

"What's going on?" Kole asked from the door.

Eiji replied, "Their bond is unique and very strong.
They're both changing because of it."

"What does that mean?" Kole questioned, clearly
concerned.

It was Eleanor who answered. "It means if they don't find Alec's purpose soon, it will kill them both."

ALEC FOUND it cathartic to get back into research. He loved detective work, making lists, and going through processes of elimination until the pieces of the puzzle fit neatly into place.

Cronin sat beside him, their sides touching at all times, as Alec went from scrolling through websites to jotting down notes on his notepad. Alec could feel the heavy weight Cronin endured, because it pressed against his chest also. They were right. Alec agreed, that the bond between him and Cronin was morphing into something else. The pull, the union between them, was getting stronger. Whatever Cronin felt, Alec felt. They could barely stand not being in the same room as each other; the anxiousness and unease was almost too much for them. And they both felt a sweet relief, a lightness of heart, when they touched. Like they could breathe again. It was incredibly intense and wonderful.

And a whole lot fucking scary.

Alec was so torn. He loved being so close to Cronin— physically, emotionally, and psychologically—he loved every second of it. But he knew in the deep recesses of his mind that it wasn't healthy to be this dependent, this psychosomatically in tune with someone else. They had a firm hold of it now, but Alec knew that spiraling out of control was just one wrong step away. There was a disconnect closing in from all sides, in the periphery. Cronin was feeling it the most, and Alec put that down to his vampire senses. Whether Alec could feel it himself or if he felt it through Cronin, he wasn't sure. Either way, it didn't matter.

They had to figure this out.

Alec looked at the webpage on Cronin's laptop and noticed that Cronin wasn't really reading it at all. He was staring into space, mentally a million miles away. Alec put his hand on Cronin's and threaded their fingers. Alec could feel the emotional burden better when he concentrated, putting names to the heaviness he felt earlier. Cronin was emanating a mix of fear and guilt, worry and inadequacy.

"Hey," Alec whispered lightly in his ear, knowing sometimes distraction was a good remedy for sullen thoughts. He nodded toward the laptop screen. "What did you find?"

"Uh," Cronin blinked a few times. "Apparently there is much hype in regards to the terracotta statues which changed formation in the British Museum yesterday."

Alec smiled at him. "I bet there is."

"No video surveillance or footage of the incidents though," Cronin said. "The soldiers turned back to statues as soon as you left apparently. Conspiracy theorists are rampant. They've closed the exhibition until further notice."

"Any credibility in the nut-job theories?" Alec asked. "Sometimes there's a little truth to the madness. Most of the time they're just tinfoil hat wearing whack jobs, but you never know. There might be a human out there who's put it all together for us."

Cronin went through the list of conspiracy theories. "UFO's are mostly to blame. Chinese government cover-ups are a close second. Ancient curses."

"They're not far wrong on that one," Alec added.

Cronin smiled. "Crop circles? Really? I do worry for the human race."

Alec snorted. "No mention of vampires or pyramidal burial grounds?"

"None."

And more and more, little by little, as Alec got Cronin to talk, the more he smiled. Alec noticed Eiji watching, and when their eyes met, Eiji grinned at him. Even Jodis had relaxed, Cronin's earlier aggression toward Eiji long forgotten. She was busy reading through old books on Chinese vampire histories, much like how Alec had studied the Egyptian histories when they were up against Keket.

But these text books weren't in English, so Alec was happy to get information secondhand. Jodis and Eiji discussed Genghis Khan, studying his life, human and vampire, much like the way Alec had uncovered background information on Keket to reveal her motives. But Alec didn't care so much for this one.

He didn't care why Genghis was doing this. Alec assumed it was world domination or some such megalomaniac nonsense. Alec was more interested in the stone plate and what exactly he had to do with it to end this whole fucking debacle.

He was tired of it. He wanted it all to be over so he could get on with living the rest of his life with Cronin. He wanted endless days of peace and fornication.

"Alec?"

"Huh?" Alec shook his head a little. Someone had asked him something. "Sorry, what?"

Cronin tilted his head. "Are you well?"

Alec loved it when Cronin asked him that. It made him smile. "Yeah, of course. I was just thinking."

"Of?"

"The things we'll do when this whole mess is over."

"Oh," Cronin said. "Any plans for us?"

Alec waggled his eyebrows. "Plenty."

Cronin gave an embarrassed laugh, his cheeks tinted the slightest pink. "That may be best left for private conversation."

"And demonstration, of course."

Eiji banged his head on the table with a groan. He mumbled something in Japanese that Alec didn't understand, but both Jodis and Cronin laughed. Alec was fairly certain that if it had been in English, the words pheromones and sexual-fucking-tension were probably said.

"So," Cronin said, steering the conversation back into safer waters. "I was asking about what information you may have found on the stone plate."

"Historical sites are in debate whether the plate actually exists," Alec started. "Some claim to have seen it. Some claim it mythical. And one thing I've learned over the last few months is that historical experts believe what they want, and facts aren't something they let get in the way of a good story."

"What do you think?" Cronin asked him.

"Well, Chinese history books were not modified like the Anglo-Saxon or Roman books were in the twelfth century. Though the stone plate predates that by almost a thousand years, "Alec stated. He sighed deeply. "In Mount Li, where the Terracotta Army was buried, there was also a tomb. It's supposedly the first Emperor of China, but I'm gonna go out on a limb here and say Genghis Khan was added to that tomb seven hundred years ago. They never found his body, and no one actually witnessed his death, if I can believe anything I've read here today."

Alec now had the attention of everyone in the house. He continued, "So, if that stone plate was in that tomb with him—which I'd bet it was—no one's seen it for *at least* seven hundred years. So that allows me to deduce that all of these Chinese history experts don't know jack shit.

"What Eleanor has seen is a stone plate with inscriptions and a center circle of some sort. I don't think the inscriptions are important. Well, not to us," Alec clarified. "They probably are to our old friend Genghis, but I can't let it get to that point. I have to stop him before then."

"How do you propose to do that?" Eiji asked.

Alec shrugged. "I'm gonna hazard a guess that I'll need to spill blood on that plate."

"Like you did in Egypt?" Cronin asked.

"Yep, though maybe this time sunlight won't rip through the room. I don't know what will happen. Maybe that's what he needs me to do so he can be the almighty powerful bastard he once was. Maybe it will give him immortality, or maybe it will turn him to dust. I really have no clue."

Cronin shook his head. "Alec, it is not like you to be so blasé. You like details and certainties. Assuming such things of our enemies will only get us killed, is that not what you said?"

Alec shrugged again. "Yes, but we have nothing to go by. We know the terracotta soldiers react to my presence. We know there's a stone plate of some sort, which relates directly to the ancient Chinese mythology of the five elements. We're guessing that I am somehow the fifth component he needs to fulfill whatever it is he's doing. What we don't know is if he needs my blood to beat us, or if we need it to beat him. We also don't know—"

Jacques put his hand up to interrupt. "The five elements will give the bearer ascension, according to ancient Chinese mythology, that is. They are the celestial rooms in which the bearer will dwell, for all eternity."

Alec sighed and rolled his eyes. He was out of patience

with this bullshit. "Yep. Immortality. Figures. Can't bad guys vie for something different these days? It's either immortality or world domination."

"Alec, are you well?" Cronin asked. Concern was clear in his eyes. "You're not acting yourself."

"I'm hungry, and I'm tired," Alec said. And he was. He didn't realize just how hungry and tired he was until he mentioned it. Actually, he was ravenous and bone weary. Yes, his days were back to front, his days were nights and vice versa, but he'd only been awake a few hours. He felt like he could sleep for a week.

In less than five seconds, Eiji had ordered a range of Japanese foods to be delivered. He'd learned so much since his first attempt at providing food, and Alec smiled as he remembered that can of refried beans that still sat in the kitchen cupboard in New York.

Alec ate everything on his plate, and no sooner had he finished, than Cronin led him out of the room and into bed.

Cronin lay down beside him, and Alec wanted to ask him when he fed last. He couldn't quite remember, and it wasn't like him to not remember, and then Alec wanted to ask Cronin about that too. But he didn't. He just needed to close his eyes for just a second, and he just needed to doze for a little while, and then he'd feel better. He meant to open his eyes, but he didn't. He slept like the dead.

AS SOON AS Alec's breaths evened out and his heart rate slowed, Cronin was out of that bed and in the living room. He didn't have to say what was on his mind—from the looks on their faces, Eiji and Jodis thought the same—but Cronin said it anyway. "Alec is not well. This has to end today."

Jodis nodded sharply. "He's behaving out of character, I agree."

Kole stood up. "What do you mean?"

"He's tired, he's apathetic, he can't remember the simplest of things," Cronin said. "It's not like him to be this way."

Eiji collected the backpacks from along the wall and upended one onto the sofa. An array of stakes and arrows splayed across the seat. "Him not caring for details was my first concern. The fact that he doesn't care as to why Genghis Khan wants him was my second concern. And he's asleep at this time?" Eiji shook his head and upended two more bags. "We need to arrange more weaponry. The fact that Alec hasn't even thought of that does not sit well with me, either."

Cronin nodded, and a cold snake of dread slithered through his belly. All of these things were true. "Not to mention his newfound ability to hear like one of us."

"Something's definitely off kilter," Jodis said. "And while he's safe and sleeping, we need to detail our plan of attack and work out contingency plans." She put her hand on Cronin's arm. "We'll make this right, Cronin. I swear it to you."

Jacques stepped forward. "Tell me what you need me to do."

So for the two hours that Alec slept, everyone made themselves busy. Jacques laid out diagrams of plans and building infrastructure of Mount Li and the huge under-ground football field-sized vaults that housed some six thou-sand terracotta soldiers. He also made lists of the locations of all Terracotta soldiers on display around the world.

Jodis spent the time on the telephone doing what she did best: outlining strategies with Kennard in England, organizing, and streamlining special operatives with the vampires who she'd recruited to join forces with them.

Eiji considered ordering more arrows and stakes online but thought it would be easier and a whole lot quicker if he Googled storage warehouses and manufacturing companies, having Cronin leap him there and just taking what they need.

Given his concern for Alec and their lack of time and planning, Cronin didn't argue. For a long moment, he listened to Alec's heartbeat, sure and steady from the bedroom where he slept, took a deep calming breath, and taking Eiji with him, they leapt.

The warehouse of the largest manufacturers of wooden arrows was in Oregon, of all places. It also happened to be nighttime there, so it was a perfect match. As soon as Cronin's feet hit the floor, the pain of absence from Alec struck him with physical force in the chest.

His human life had ended with an axe to his breastbone, and the pain—the way it made him stagger and suck back air—felt almost the same.

Eiji grabbed Cronin, steadying him, while Cronin pushed the heel of his hand against his sternum. He gasped like each breath was a blow. "Eiji, hurry."

Eiji turned, scanning for mass supplies of arrows as he ran. All Cronin could do was stand there, leaning against a sorting machine of some type with his hands on his knees, gritting his teeth through the pain.

This wasn't good. This was too much. And Cronin knew if he felt this, then Alec did too, sleeping be damned. There was no way he could sleep through this.

Eiji came back with his arms full of arrows, just as Cronin heard it.

Cronin, please. Please.

CHAPTER THIRTEEN

IT TOOK every ounce of his strength to stand to his full height. Still with one hand against his heart, he reached out for Eiji with his other hand, and took them back to the only place Cronin's body and mind would take him.

Back to Alec.

And Alec stood, surrounded by Kole and Jodis with concern on their faces. Cronin had no sooner arrived back in the living room, than he ran to Alec and embraced him. Finally, both men breathed.

"Don't do that again," Alec gasped.

"I know," Cronin mumbled into Alec's neck. "Apologies, m'cridhe. I did not intend to wake you."

"Alec woke up screaming," Jodis said.

"Cronin could barely stand," Eiji told her. "His absence from Alec literally knocked him off his feet."

Cronin pressed his forehead to Alec's neck, his collarbone, as he pulled back a little. Alec still fisted his shirt, so he couldn't get too far. "I'll not leave you again."

"Can someone explain what the hell is going on?" Kole snapped. "What the hell was that?"

"When fated couples first meet, they experience an intensity, a notice of absence when they're parted," Jodis explained. "It normally fades after a few months."

"But Alec and Cronin are getting worse," Eiji added, putting his burden of arrows on the sofa. "Alec, whatever we need you to do, we need you to do it sooner rather than later."

Alec nodded, still gripping onto Cronin's shirt. "Okay." He took a deep breath and looked at both Jodis and Eiji. "I think I have a plan. Or part of it. I don't know." He uncurled his fingers from Cronin's shirt and put his hand to Cronin's face. "Though I don't think you'll like it too much."

"What is it?"

"Well, I was thinking about what we need to end this Genghis Khan thing and something that Eleanor said," Alec told them. "We need my blood to stop him somehow, and Eleanor said I fall sick. So what I thought was, I should have blood taken. If you guys all carry a vial or bag of it, then if I'm out of action, you can still take Khan down without me."

A low and livid growl rumbled in Cronin's chest. No, he didn't like the idea too much at all. Any of it. The thought of someone taking Alec's blood, *or* that he would be taken too ill to do it himself. "Alec," he warned.

Alec put his palm to Cronin's chest, directly above his heart. "It's the only plan B we've got. It's logical. I'm not being some self-sacrificing martyr, but we need to look at the bigger picture." He frowned. "I'm not stupid, Cronin. I know something's not right with me, and I know you feel it too. But this isn't about us. This is about taking out some psycho before he eradicates half a billion people in Asia."

"I can't bear the thought," Cronin said, his voice cracking.

"I know. But it's just a contingency plan," Alec said soothingly. He slid his hand from Cronin's chest up to cup his cheek. "We need to do this right, to end it once and for all. We have forever on the other side of this. Isn't that worth it?"

Cronin leaned into Alec's palm and closed his eyes, aware this intimate moment between them was in front of everyone else, but he couldn't bring himself to care. He gave a nod, silently agreeing, and Alec tilted Cronin's face upward so he could press his lips to his before embracing him. Then, over the top of Cronin's head, Alec laughed and asked, "So, anyone here skilled at taking blood?"

"Your attempt at humor is not funny," Cronin said as his growl got louder.

Alec squeezed him and kissed the side of his head with smiling lips. "I wouldn't let anyone else even try."

CRONIN REFUSED to go anywhere without Alec, so given they needed supplies outside of what the nearest Japanese town would allow, it required leaping.

Eiji went with them, refusing to let them go alone. Their first stop was a medical supply warehouse, second stop was for human food. They chose a grocery store that had closed for the night and collected some bread, milk, eggs, meat, and enough fruits and vegetables to last both Alec and Kole a few days.

Alec added some nashi pears to his cart when Eiji came back with a canister of white powder, looking pleased with himself. "What is that?" Alec asked.

"It is used for gelling tofu," Eiji said.

Alec made a face. "Well, rest assured there won't be any need for tofu-gelling in my dietary requirements."

Eiji laughed but didn't put the canister back. Then Alec thought of something. Somewhere along the way, he'd lost track of days. He looked to Cronin and asked, "When was the last time you ate?"

"I'm fine," he replied.

"That wasn't my question."

Cronin sighed. "I've gone longer without feeding, Alec. I will be fine."

Alec growled in frustration. "Eiji, can you please tell him he needs to feed."

Eiji's smile slowly slid away. "Alec, he cannot leave you, and you cannot go with him to feed. Given he is lacking in options, abstinence is his only alternative."

"I can't have him starving," Alec argued. "It jeopardizes everything: agility, cognitive function, not to mention his comfort."

"Alec, I said I'm fine," Cronin repeated sharply.

"You could leap us to a dark city somewhere. I'll wait on the street. You go into an alley or something. I'll be just a few feet away," Alec suggested.

"You would not be bothered to bear witness to such a thing?" Eiji asked.

Alec knew it was wrong, callous, and just a touch psychotic; his policing vow to serve and protect was not aimed at the community any more. It was aimed solely and directly at Cronin. "He could slaughter a whole fucking village and I wouldn't care, as long as it meant he wasn't hungry."

Eiji snorted. "Alec, any concerns I've had at how you'll take to being one of us are unfounded. I think you'll be just fine."

Alec let his head fall back and he sighed at the ceiling of the grocery store. "I don't *want* a whole village to die, just so you know." Then he looked squarely at Cronin. "I rather like the idea of ridding the streets of murderers and rapists, but putting my teeth to someone's throat and drinking his blood might be another story all together."

Cronin stood in front of him and cupped his face gently. "Oh, Alec. Don't let it weigh on your mind prematurely."

Just then the blue and red lights of a police car flashed through the opaque glass at the front of the store. "That concludes our shopping trip for today, boys and girls," Eiji said, throwing a few more things into their stash of stolen goods.

Alec gave a wave to the security cameras, tossed a bunch of money on the counter as thanks, and with a simple touch from Cronin they were gone.

———

ALEC TOOK the medical supplies into the bedroom he'd slept in. If Cronin was going to take his blood with a needle, doing it in front of a half dozen vampires probably wasn't a great idea. Alec had suggested they leap somewhere private, but Cronin had assured him it would be fine.

"No one will come near me," he said simply. "Unless they'd like it to be the last thing they ever did."

Eiji and Jodis just laughed, but Eleanor and Jacques decided it would be best if they weren't present. "We'll take a late night stroll into town," Eleanor said. She was mindful of what was said in front of Kole, and the two seemed to enjoy each other's company. They were playing chess when Alec, Cronin, and Eiji got back, with Sammy the cat purring loudly at Eleanor's side. They looked rather comfortable together, Alec thought.

And when Eleanor left, Kole stood up and stretched. "And I'll be heading off to bed," he said. "I've been disgraced as a chess player by a woman who cannot even see, so if you don't mind, I'll take what's left of my pride and go to bed."

Alec gave his dad a smile. "Good night."

When his father was gone, Alec saw that Eiji was at the table dipping each arrow head and stake into a liquid goo. "Hey, Eij. Whatcha doing?"

"I'm modifying each weapon to combat the Terracotta Army."

"How?"

"Well, the terracotta used to make this army is clay based."

"And?"

"Are you familiar with chemistry and physics?"

"A little. Basic high school stuff." He inspected the white gooey paste. "Is that your tofu gelling stuff?"

"Yes."

Alec looked at the wooden arrows and stakes. "Um, Eij, I hate to be the one to break it to you, but you're not gelling tofu."

Eiji laughed long and loud. "Oh, Alec. You make me laugh." He held up one arrow, letting the white goo drip thickly back into the bowl. "So you know clay minerals are characterized by two-dimensional sheets of corner sharing SiO_4 tetrahedra, or AlO_4 octahedra. Sometimes both."

Alec blinked slowly.

"These sheets have the chemical composition $(Al,Si)_3O_4$. Each silica tetrahedron shares three of its vertex oxygen atoms—"

Alec put his hand up, then scratched his head. "Eiji, stop. You lost me at the word clay. I said I did basic high-school chemistry. I am not Einstein, my friend. I'm gonna need that in English."

Eiji chuckled. "Clay found in the Indo-China area is high in salt."

"Okay," Alec nodded. "Now that I understood."

"So salt, or sodium chloride, is an ionic compound, yes?"

Alec stared. "Uh, I have no clue, so I'm just gonna go with a yes because you said it was."

Eiji's smile widened. "But salts in clay can be broken down or dissolved when mixed with a compound that has the exact opposite electrical charge."

Alec scratched his head. "Uh, okay. Can we get to the point without the chemistry and physics lesson?"

Eiji held up an arrow that had been dipped in the paste and showed him the tip. "If we apply a compound that immediately attacks the sodium molecules within the clay, it will cause the clay platelets to relax or fall away from each other."

"It will break down the clay?"

Eiji nodded proudly. "Yes."

"Well, that's great and all, Eiji," Alec said. And it was. In theory. "But I thought we'd go in with a much simpler line of attack."

Eiji tilted his head. "What's that?"

"A sledgehammer."

Cronin and Jodis laughed, and Eiji grinned. "It's not as scientific as my theory, Alec, but I do believe it to be just as effective."

Alec picked up the bowl of goo and smelled it. "I like the principle of your idea though. Maybe we should spray them with this shit when we're done smashing them to make sure they never come back."

"Good idea," Eiji said with a laugh.

"Well," Jodis said, changing the subject. "I think it might be a good idea if Eiji and I wait until Jacques and Eleanor return, then we might leave to feed also."

Cronin gave a nod. "Agreed."

"And Cronin?" Alec asked. "When will he feed?"

"Alec," Cronin said softly. He walked over to him and put his hands to his face. "Please don't be concerned. If I say I am fine, then you must believe me."

Alec sighed and leaned his face into Cronin's palm. "I worry for you, that's all."

"I know you do. I can feel it," he whispered.

Jodis was sorting through arrows, and Eiji looked busy online now ordering sledgehammers, so Alec gave Cronin a pointed nod to the hall that led to the bedrooms. Alec walked into the bedroom and collected the medical supplies he'd put there earlier. Cronin was half a step behind him. He whispered, a vampire-quiet whisper, so Eiji and Jodis wouldn't hear given they were three rooms away. "I know you said it's safe, but I'd rather not do the blood draw here. Can we leap somewhere?"

The briefest confusion flickered in Cronin's eyes, but he collected himself. "Whatever you prefer." He touched the side of Alec's face with just his fingertips. "Alec? You seem quite out of sorts. Is something wrong? You would tell me if you weren't feeling well?"

"I'm okay, I think," Alec replied, equally as quiet. "I don't know how I feel. I just have another plan B."

ALEC WAS surprised Cronin took him back to the New York City apartment. They arrived in the bathroom, Alec assumed because if there was an unwanted vampire waiting for someone to arrive, they wouldn't wait in the bathroom. Cronin was stock still, listening, then he smelled the air. "It's clear," he said. "There hasn't been anyone here since we left."

Alec exhaled loudly, relief coursing through him. "Thank God." He went into the bedroom and threw the backpack with medical supplies on the bed. "I love this place. I'd hate to never live here again."

Cronin smiled warmly. "I thought you were fond of your studio, not this luxury apartment."

Alec laughed. "And you said you hated sarcasm. For something you don't like, you use a lot of it." Alec looked around at the huge, lavish bedroom, the opulent furniture, and finally to the ax and helmet, which took pride of place on the only shelf in the room. Next to it now sat the sun-disk of Ra, Alec's souvenir of his battle in Egypt. "It's not the luxury I love here. I mean, it's nice, don't get me wrong. But it's because you're here. Your belongings, the things you hold dear. It feels like you." Even in the darkened room, Alec could see Cronin blush a little. He cupped his cheek to feel the spread of warmth there. "Will this always be our home?"

Cronin's eyes fluttered closed and he gasped in a quiet breath. Cronin took a moment before speaking. "It thrills me still to hear you say such words. *Our home.* I'd not have believed two simple words could steal my breath."

Alec swiped the pad of his thumb across Cronin's cheek and leaned in so he could kiss him, just softly on the lips. "I love the way you talk."

Cronin chuckled. "How so?"

"Well, I'm all twenty-first century, slang words, zero respect for the English language, or any language for that matter. And you speak so properly, so perfectly. It's like each sentence is a gift."

Cronin's eyes widened, as did his smile. "A gift? Did you bring me here to flatter me? Because if you thought you'd need to pander me with sycophancy just to bed me, you needn't have gone to so much trouble."

Alec laughed. "Now you're just showing off. Sycophancy? Really? I'm pretty sure that word hasn't been used in day-to-day conversation in a few hundred years. Does a brain become a thesaurus during the vampire change?"

Cronin ignored the jibe. "The mind is broadened exponentially, but prior intelligence is an advantage. You will be more than fine. Actually, perhaps your mind—given you have vampire tendencies already—will be exceptional."

"Will you tell me what else happens?" Alec asked quietly. "What will happen to me?"

Cronin put his hand to Alec's face and pushed a wayward strand of hair back. "I'm not expecting your change to be typical," he started. His voice was soft and soothing. "Considering your inability to change when bitten before, I would expect you to be anything but conventional." Cronin was quiet for a long moment, and Alec had wondered if that was all he was going to say. "There will be pain, Alec. Your cells, your very DNA, bodily organs, circulatory system, nervous system all change, and it burns and shreds you. The metamorphosis is not easy, and I wish I could bear it for you."

Alec swallowed hard. "How long does it take?"

"Normally, a full day. Twenty-four hours." Cronin frowned deeply. "It might not sound like a long time, but it will be an eternity for you. You will beg for death."

Now Alec cupped Cronin's face. "If I do? Promise you won't listen to me, no matter how much I beg." Then Alec realized something. "What will happen to you when I'm... changing? Fated couples feel each other's pain, yes? But no vampire has ever been fated with a human, so no vampire has had to endure watching them change."

"Only you would think of such a thing." Cronin smiled sadly. "I don't know how I will endure it. No one knows. But have no concern for me, my love. You will have enough to endure. What I'll be going through will be like a spring evening on the moors compared to the walk through hell you'll be taking."

"I'll endure it a hundred times over if it means I get forever with you," Alec said, kissing him softly again. "It's just a means to an end for me, if that makes sense. Like I just need one door to close so another can open."

"You mean, you need your life to end."

"One life," Alec replied simply. "So my next life can start."

Cronin shook his head incredulously. "You are a confounding man. Though we've established your blood is different, *you* are different, so your change to vampire will not be a predictable one."

Alec nodded and took a deep breath, not really knowing how Cronin would react to this. "That's what I wanted to talk to you about. My other plan B."

"What is it?"

"Well, when you drank my blood, it gave you the ability of vampires around you, right?"

Cronin's brow knitted and he nodded. "Yes. It was highly irregular and most disconcerting. Why, Alec?"

Alec was sure Cronin knew what was coming next, but he laid it all out anyway. "I think you should drink from me again." He put his hands up before Cronin could object. "Hear me out, please." Alec took Cronin's hand and sat on the bed. He looked up at him and took a slow breath. "It's not for gratification or because I find it hot or because I need you to bite me. I mean, all of those things might be a little bit true, but it's more than that. I think you should drink from me, take my blood so you can very deliberately transfer the powers of those around you."

"Alec," Cronin shook his head.

"Let me finish, please." Alec pulled on Cronin's hand and waited for him to sit beside him. "We have no clue what we're facing. We don't know what Khan's powers are or who he has with him. We don't know what the Terracotta Army are capable of, but if you have the ability to use their own powers against them or even just to warn us as to what they are, then we stand a better chance."

Cronin was quiet for a while, obviously thinking about what Alec was saying. "I can see it would be beneficial if it went to plan. But it would carry its own risks. Not just to me but to everyone I take with me. If I get disoriented—to be in someone else's head is overpowering, Alec—I put everyone else at risk because, what if I'm not capable of leaping us all out of there? I won't jeopardize you like that."

Well, Alec hadn't thought of that. "Fair enough. But when you experienced it before, you didn't know what it was. Now we do. It won't be a shock. In fact, you'll be looking for it."

"I don't know how to use other powers," Cronin said, shaking his head.

"You might not have to *use* them," Alec countered. "But if we get there and Genghis has some guards with powers, you'll know what we're up against at least. I think it would work, Cronin. I know you worry about others, but I have complete faith in you to do it. Actually, you're the only one who I think *could* do it."

Cronin made a face but he didn't argue, and Alec knew he was almost won over.

"I think it could be the ace up our sleeve. Our secret. Not even Jodis or Eiji would know, and—"

"I won't keep it from them," Cronin said. "I cannot lie to them, Alec."

Alec lifted Cronin's hand to his lips and kissed his knuckles. "You are a man of integrity. Okay, so we tell them. I'd say Eleanor has seen this conversation anyway, or at least my decision to put it to you."

"What if your blood is more potent now than what it was before?" Cronin asked. "What if it—"

"What if it works?" Alec countered. "What if it's how we win? Eleanor always said I was *Cronin's key*. What if she meant I was the key, or my blood at least, to you being the one who saves us."

Cronin sighed heavily. "You're convinced, aren't you?"

"Yes."

"And I have little to no chance of convincing you otherwise?"

"Correct."

"And that's why you wanted to not do the blood draw in the company of others?" he asked. "And allow me to feed."

"You are a smart man," Alec said. He stood up and unbuttoned his jeans, pushing them down to the floor, underpants and all. He stepped out of the denim, lifted his right leg to the foot of the bed and let his cock hang thick and heavy in front of Cronin. He gave himself a few long, languid strokes, knowing Cronin would also see the line of fading purple puncture marks on his inner thigh, and Alec bit back a groan when Cronin licked his lips. "Femoral or carotid?"

Alec found himself on his back in the middle of the bed with Cronin fixed well between his thighs. He licked the length of Alec's cock, sucking good and hard before tonguing his balls and the silky skin of his inner thigh. Alec put his hands through his hair and closed his eyes, savoring every sensation. "Femoral it is, then," he mumbled.

Cronin was purring and growling, a wicked sound that unleashed pleasure in Alec's belly. He jerked Alec's cock, twisting his hand over the glans, just the way Alec liked it. He teased his hole with his tongue and fingers, working both hands over him, quickly bringing Alec to the edge. Then when Alec was on the brink, when it was all too much and he couldn't hold it back another second, Cronin sunk his fangs into Alec's inner thigh, and Alec came.

Alec's world had barely righted itself when Cronin, cock in hand, pressing it against Alec's hole, was asking for permission. "Alec?"

Alec groaned, and reached for Cronin blindly, pulling him closer. "God, yes," he mumbled. Alec knew his duty as *the key* was coming to an end soon, and if this was his last time to lay with Cronin as a human, he wanted him inside him. Filling him, fucking him, owning every inch of him, and finally pulsing and coming inside him.

Completion.

Alec understood now what that really meant. It wasn't some prudish, polite way to describe an orgasm. It was to be at one with Cronin, to be whole, to be complete.

To be fated.

Alec put his hands to Cronin's face, taking in his lust-drunk eyes and vampire teeth behind his lazy smile. "You're so perfect," Alec murmured and brought their lips together.

Eventually Cronin broke their kiss to moan. "My head is swimming."

"In a good way?" Alec asked.

"Such a good way," Cronin said with a bit of a laugh. "Your blood is the purest form I've ever tasted."

"What will you do when I'm changed to a vampire?" Alec asked with a smile. "I won't be human. There'll be no more."

Cronin laughed and shook his head slowly. "To the contrary. I'll have it forever."

"You can still drink vampire blood?"

"Only from your fated one."

"Really?"

Cronin slipped out of Alec and quickly rolled so they were on their sides, their arms around each other. He pulled the covers over them, which Alec knew Cronin did as a gesture for him. "Well, there is a lot of intimacy between vampire couples. And that means a lot of biting."

Alec hummed contentedly. "Does that mean I'll get to bite you?"

Cronin moaned loudly. "I should hope so."

Alec remembered how Cronin reacted to him nipping at the skin on his neck before, and he laughed. "I can't wait to taste you."

Cronin shivered from head to foot, and his breath caught. "As I can't wait to be tasted."

They lay like that for a long while, tracing absent-minded circles on skin with dreamy fingers, though Alec knew a deadline loomed. Eventually he sighed. "I guess we should do the bloodsucking thing."

Cronin chuckled low in Alec's ear. "Don't move." Cronin grabbed the backpack that had fallen off the bed. "Why do you presume me to even know how to do this?"

Alec snorted. "Well, I figure it's inserting a sharp object into a vein to draw blood—my blood—so that would make you an expert."

One corner of Cronin's lips curled in a half-smile. "I've never done it *this* way before."

"We can go back to Doctor Benavides if you'd prefer."

Cronin gave a low, threatening growl as his answer.

Alec chuckled. "Yep. That's what I thought." Still lying on his back on the bed, Alec inspected the crook of his elbow, tapping it for a vein. "It should be easy enough. I never had problems giving blood before."

This time it was Cronin who laughed. "Your blood flow is exceptional." Cronin took Alec's arm and ran his fingertips over the crease in Alec's arm. "Here," he said, stopping at a precise point. "The vein is just under here."

"You can feel that?"

"Of course." Cronin gave a shrug. "Feel it, hear it, sense it. It is as though all of my senses are drawn to the easiest access of release."

"Oh."

Cronin laughed. "Shall we start?"

"Yep."

Cronin disappeared briefly into the walk in closet and came back out wearing new clothes and holding a necktie. He sat on the edge of the bed. "You'll need this around the top of your bicep to act as a tourniquet," he said, tying it off tightly. Cronin frowned at the homemade strap around Alec's arm. "Is this comfortable?"

"It's fine," Alec said, squeezing his hand into a fist over and over. With his other hand, he tucked the covers around his waist and kept his arm extended out near the edge of the bed while Cronin unpacked the half-pint blood bags. They were the ones used in hospitals and clinics. Alec had seen them a thousand times. Small, rounded, white-clear pouches with IV kits attached.

Cronin handled them expertly. He may have never done this before, but he was an intelligent man. After looking at all the pieces, he seemed to know which IV lines went where, how to use a cannula, and what clamps went where. "Are you sure?" Cronin asked one more time.

Alec gave him a kind smile. "Yes."

Cronin slid the needle against the now-protruding vein, piercing the skin expertly. He attached the IV line to the cannula and blood started to flow through the tube and the bag began to fill.

"Are you well?" Cronin asked softly.

Alec always smiled when Cronin asked him that. "I feel good. Great, actually. You know, I think this bloodletting is making me better. You drinking from me made me better. Remember how I was fuzzy-headed and tired before? Well, that's gone now."

Cronin frowned. "You were suffering for my sake. I don't like that."

Alec rubbed his back with his free hand. "How were we to know? And anyways, it won't matter after this is over. I'll be a vampire, won't I?"

Cronin was quiet for a while and seemed to find the bedroom carpet fascinating. "Will you regret it?" he whispered.

Alec laughed at that. "Never."

"You will leave your humanity behind, by choice, Alec. That's not something to take lightly."

"I don't take it lightly. You know, twelve months ago when I was just Alec MacAidan, New York Detective, living a semi-normal life, I would have said no." Cronin met Alec's gaze with a look of fire and confusion. Alec held out his free hand and waited for Cronin to take it. He couldn't help but smile. "But I'm not that Alec anymore. Since I met you, I'm different, in the very best of ways. Now, I couldn't not be a vampire. I couldn't not have forever with you."

Cronin smiled in return. "Your words warm my heart. Though I still wish you didn't have to sacrifice anything. I wish to give you the world, not take things away."

"You're not taking anything away," Alec replied. "You're giving me everything."

Cronin squeezed his hand before bringing it to his lips and kissing Alec's knuckles. "Don't misread my melancholy. I want nothing more than for you to join me in this life, though I will lament the loss of your humanity, Alec. How could I not?"

Alec wasn't sure what to say to that. Because really, what words were there to cover such a thing? Instead, Alec squeezed Cronin's hand and redirected the conversation. "You know what I'll miss the most when I'm not human?"

"What's that?"

"Sunshine. Not that I saw a lot of it. I mean I worked night shift in New York City. Even in broad daylight, the buildings shielded most of it, but I think it will be the age-old problem of wanting something you can't have," Alec said. "Or steak. An inch thick prime fillet, medium rare," Alec hummed. "I can't decide which one I'll miss more."

Cronin smiled at that. "Trust me, human food will not interest you. But if you wish, we can select your favorite meals and you can have them until its time."

"Sounds great!" Alec chuckled. "Having a last supper. How very Jesus of me."

Cronin laughed quietly, then set about changing the blood bag. He got Alec juice and a sandwich from the kitchen to replenish his sugar levels, or so Cronin had said.

He was clearly concerned with the amount of blood Alec
was giving, but Alec reassured him every time that he felt
great. When the third half-pint bag was done, Cronin
attached the fourth and last bag, and Cronin was insistent
on feeding Alec more food and juice, Alec thought it might
be a good time to ask him something that had weighed on
his mind for a while.

"Can I ask you something?"

"Of course."

"What will I be like?" Alec asked. "I mean, what can I
expect after I'm changed?"

Cronin gave him a small smile. "I wondered when you
would ask this." Alec waited for him to continue. Cronin
played with Alec's fingers for a moment and exhaled loudly.
"You will be different. Eleanor has seen it, citing your
powers as a human for the reason you will acquire great
power in your vampire life, and I agree with her theory. I
cannot say for certain what your experience will be like. If
your powers will make the transition any different, we have
no way of knowing. I've told you before of the actual
changing process: it burns and pulls and stretches every cell
in your body. That process is the same for everyone, regardless of the talents they acquire upon transition, so I imagine
that will not change for you."

Cronin paused a moment. Alec knew Cronin was loath
for him to experience any kind of pain, but at the end of the
day, it was inevitable. Alec squeezed his hand, a silent reas-
surance, and urged him to continue.

"The days that follow your change will be difficult, but
in the sense of hunger and being disoriented. Every sense
you have now will be increased exponentially, and theoreti-
cally that sounds great, though in practice it's something
else altogether. Your speed and strength will take getting

used to, as will your balance. You will essentially need to learn how to walk again."

"From scratch?"

Cronin snorted. "No, not from scratch. But to walk in measured, slow, human steps takes a concerted effort, considering your body will want to expend energy in ways you cannot imagine. It's best not be around humans for the first few weeks at least, not just because you'll want to drain them dry, but because your movements will either look too fast, or too erratic as you attempt to pull your abilities back."

Alec swallowed hard. "Will I," he asked quietly, "want to drain everyone dry?"

Cronin held his stare for a long while. "Yes."

Alec nodded slowly. His voice was a mumbled whisper, "Yeah, I figured as much."

"Still not having regrets?" Cronin asked, as if daring him.

Alec met his gaze with nothing but sincerity and deter-mination. "Never."

Cronin smiled widely and kissed Alec's knuckles again. "How are you feeling? Light headed? Dizzy? You've lost quite a lot of blood, more than should be allowed for a human. Your heart rate is good," he noted. Then he put his fingers to Alec's pulse and listened for a few seconds. "Your blood pressure is normal. Are you sure you don't feel affected?"

Alec shook his head. "I told you, I feel great. Better than great. I think letting half my blood out helped or something. I don't know. And anyway, you can tell my blood pressure by listening?"

Cronin snorted. "Anything to do with your health or your blood is like a beacon to me."

Alec grinned at him. "So, you're like my personal physician?"

"Not likely, no."

"That's a shame," Alec teased. "Because there's a lot of doctor/patient rules I'd love to break with you."

Cronin laughed and shook his head. "I don't think physical exercise would be wise for you right now. You've just lost two pints of blood, Alec. Not to mention what I took from your thigh before. That's enough to kill a human, yet you say you feel great?"

"Much better. And really? No exercise?" Alec huffed and gave Cronin his best pout. Cronin just smiled at him and set about clamping off the last bag of blood. Only when he removed the cannula, blood pooled on Alec's skin, making Cronin hiss.

He quickly covered the needle mark to stop the flow, but Alec pulled his hand away. "Alec," he growled, low and warning.

Alec bit back a groan. He grabbed the bag of blood, including the still-attached IV line and let a thin trail of his blood drip across his chest.

Cronin bared his fangs, his eyes turned to molten onyx and he growled.

The sight and sound of Cronin without restraint made Alec moan. He let the bag of blood fall to the bed and slowly, purposefully, with his eyes locked on Cronin's, he drew his finger through the blood and put it to his mouth.

A snarl ripped through the air. "You shouldn't tempt me like that, Alec," he growled.

Alec's whole body thrummed, pleasure buzzed through his veins and pooled in his groin. He'd never seen Cronin so... *vampire* before. His eyes were sharp and focused, his teeth were bared and ready, he slinked low, like he was ready to pounce up Alec's half-naked body. He looked feral with hunger for blood and sex, and Alec felt lightning in his veins.

He'd never been so aroused, every one of his senses were piqued. Thrill, arousal, fear, and desire. He wanted it.

He licked his bloodstained finger and Cronin growled more menacingly, and ripped the bed sheet from Alec's body. The unbridled power felt like a jolt straight to his cock, and Cronin crawled up his naked form, licking the trail of blood from Alec's skin and pushing his thighs apart with his own. His hard cock was at Alec's hole, still slicked with come from before. "Your blood belongs to me," he snarled.

Alec's back arched and his cock pulsed, and precome spilled out freely into his navel. "If you want it," Alec writhed, "then come get it."

Cronin pushed his hips up into Alec, penetrating him, hard and fast, and sunk his teeth into Alec's neck at the same time. He fucked as he drank, a closed circuit of pure ecstasy. Alec's whole body convulsed, impaled at both ends, and unable to contain the pleasure, he came.

ALEC WAS STILL LAUGHING when they leapt back to the house in Japan. They'd left the bedroom in a mess of a deconstructed bed and ripped clothes. And as soon as they'd arrived, Jodis and Eiji knew what they'd done.

Alec didn't try to hide the puncture marks on his neck. He just grinned at them and put the backpack on the table.

"Cronin," Jodis started, "I thought we agreed until we knew how it affected you—"

"It wasn't Cronin's decision," Alec stated plainly. "It was mine."

All the vampires turned to him and waited for him to explain.

"The effects drinking my blood has on Cronin could be beneficial when we go to take down the Terracotta Army. If he can predetermine what other talents are against us, then we hold the advantage. If he can transfer their talent and use it against them, even better." Alec opened the backpack and took out the first of the blood bags. "And it appears bloodletting fixes me. Like it releases pressure or something. I don't feel foggy anymore. I can actually think straight."

Eiji snorted. "Well, not too straight." He sniffed the air. "There wasn't anything *straight* about what you two were doing."

Alec laughed and put the other blood bags next to the first. "And we showered and everything."

Cronin put a protective hand on Alec's back. He was fighting a smile. "Alec feels much better."

"I bet he does," Jodis said. She rolled her eyes and grinned at Cronin. "And those are the blood pouches?"

"Yep. Little juice boxes for vampires," Alec answered. "Four of them with half a pint each."

Eiji laughed at his joke. No one else did. "Alec," Jacques said. "That's a lot of blood loss."

"Not to mention what Cronin had," Alec said with a laugh. "And I've never felt better."

"This is all very concerning," Jodis murmured. Alec wasn't sure if he was supposed to hear it, but he could hear everything.

Cronin nodded. "It's not typical human behavior, no."

"It's not even human anatomy," Jodis replied. "He should be dead."

"I feel great," Alec repeated. "I feel amazing actually."

No one spoke for a long time, so Alec studied the white-board. There'd been a few more points added, a few research details but nothing major. Eiji stood beside him and, trying not to be observing him too obviously, said, "So now you're feeling so well, did you want to do some research?"

Alec shrugged non-committedly.

Eiji rocked back on his heels, going for nonchalance. "When we went to Egypt, you were all about researching hieroglyphs and background information, being prepared and learning everything you could."

Alec hummed. "Yes, but this one feels different."

Cronin was quick to question. "How so?"

"I don't know exactly. Like something is not what it seems."

This time Jodis asked, "Alec, what do you mean?"

"Something's not right," he said again, more adamant this time. "Like Genghis Khan and his Terracotta Army are a ruse."

"You've seen Terracotta Soldiers move in front of you," Eiji said. "Do you doubt their existence?"

"No, no," Alec answered quickly. "They're real alright. I just think there's more to it than just Genghis Khan. I just feel that all along we've been asking the wrong questions. I want to know why Genghis Khan hasn't called for me yet? If he needs me so badly, why is he waiting? How does he know I'll even turn up? But more importantly, I want to know who's behind it. Who brought Genghis Khan back from the dead? That's who we need to find. I think we need to go back and see Jorge again."

Eleanor came running into the room with Kole. "Something just changed!" she said. Then she spun around to the far wall. "Incoming!"

And then, as though right on cue, another Chinese warrior appeared in their living room. Though he was dressed for battle, this one bore no weapons. Only a smile. He held out his hand and disappeared, leaving whatever it was he was holding to fall to the floor.

Cronin had his arms around Alec, ready to leap, when Eiji went over and picked up what the uninvited leaper had dropped. He held out his hand and showed them.

Alec recognized it immediately. "It's my old watch. I gave it to Jorge."

"You wanted to know how Genghis will lure you there, and now you know," Eleanor said. "They have the vampire child. And they know you will come for him."

CHAPTER FOURTEEN

"WE DON'T KNOW ENOUGH," Cronin argued. "Alec, I can't just leap you there without knowing what will be waiting for us."

Alec put the backpack on and picked up the night vision goggles he'd used in Egypt and put them with one of the sledgehammers Eiji had bought. "What will welcome us is about five thousand terracotta vampires. I assume Genghis Khan will have guards with talents that more than likely include some kind of masonry skills, given this is all about clay and stone. I would also expect Genghis to have some kind of skill of influence. He wants me to complete some circle of power, for world domination or to control the elements or what-the-fuck-ever. It doesn't matter."

"How does it not matter?" Cronin cried. Everyone else stood in silence and watched them bicker.

"Because he's not the one behind this," Alec argued. "I don't know how I know that, I just do. He's just a pawn in this."

Cronin shook his head. "Even so, a humble pawn can

checkmate a king, Alec. Do not underestimate an ancient vampire with a thirst for revenge."

"Who do you think is orchestrating this?" Jodis asked.

Alec shrugged. "The same person who turned Tahini Shafiq into the Egyptian vampire Queen Keket. The same person who used the dreams of my parents to give me my name. Maybe what Mikka said in the alley before he died had a double meaning. He said "it's not one, it's both". Maybe he knew something we don't. Maybe he'd clued in on something and died before he could tell any of you."

Jacques shook his head. "I was with him that night. I didn't see anything."

"Maybe he did. I don't know," Alec countered. He put the heel of his hand against his sternum. "I just feel it, right here. There's someone else, some*thing* else. And it ends tonight." He held up the last remaining bulletproof vest to Cronin. He was the only one who hadn't put one on yet. "Please put this on."

Cronin took the vest. "And your protection is what?"

"You," Alec answered. He held up the sledgehammer. "And this."

"Alec," Kole started. "Son, I...."

Alec put the hammer down and took four long strides over to his father, and hugged him. "I love you, Dad."

"Love you too, Ailig." Kole choked back tears and swallowed thickly. He pulled back and took a deep breath. "You're not coming back, are you?"

Alec couldn't lie to him. "Not human, no."

Kole nodded quickly and tears brimmed in his eyes. "But I'll see you again?"

"Maybe not right away, Dad," Alec said. "But soon. I promise."

Eiji, who had been on the phone to Kennard, clicked off

the call. "They'll meet us here," he said, pointing at the map on the whiteboard, and more specifically he pointed to the largest hangar-like warehouse that housed the Terracotta Army. "At the top of the hour."

Alec looked at his new watch. They had ten minutes. He pulled out his pistol and double-checked the magazine. He only had a handful of wooden bullets left from when they'd fought in Egypt. He hadn't bothered ordering anymore, guessing they'd be useless against vampires made of terracotta. He also guessed he was about to discover a new way to kill a vampire tonight. Sure, a wooden stake or bullet to the heart worked just fine, but smashing a terra-cotta vampire into pulverized dust with a sledgehammer would be just as effective.

He did, however, still opt to carry wooden stakes and two pistols loaded with the last of his wooden-tipped bullets, because there was every chance non-terracotta vampires would also be there. Like Genghis Khan himself. Or the one who created him.

Alec made sure his thigh holster and quiver were securely fastened and that Cronin, Jodis, Eiji, and Jacques each had their pouch of his blood in their backpacks. That was his only contingency plan: if his blood was required to end Genghis Khan, then any one of them were armed to do it. That and the fact Cronin could transfer or at least sense the talents of other vampires, were the only two aces up their sleeves. Alec just hoped it was enough.

Alec fixed one of the fasteners on Cronin's vest that didn't really need fixing. He pulled the strap tight before patting it down, and when he was done, the two men stared at each other.

Alec could see a storm of emotions in Cronin's eyes, and

it hurt him to see it. Alec put his hand to Cronin's face. "We'll get through this."

"Your complacency concerns me," Cronin whispered.

"It's not complacency," Alec told him. "I don't know how to describe how I feel. It's a sense of calm. Like I know I'm about to get all the answers to every question we've asked." Alec kissed his lips. "I am ready for this."

Eiji, Jodis, and Jacques stood is a sort of circle in the middle of the living room, waiting for Cronin and Alec to join them in formation. But before they leapt anywhere, Alec felt the need to say a few words.

"Listen guys, I just wanted to say it's been an honor and a privilege. While our main objective is to take out Genghis and get Jorge back, it's not worth any of us dying. I'd like to look back in a thousand years and laugh about this with all of you." Alec looked pointedly at Eiji. "No self-sacrificing bullshit this time, you hear? And, if Cronin's not near me when I'm hit or injured, or whatever it is that Eleanor sees that reverses my inability to be changed into a vampire, I give permission for any of one of you to change me." Alec turned to Cronin, ignoring his death stare and low growl. "I'd prefer to have you pissed off at me for the next few hundred years than not have any years with you at all, if you know what I mean. If I need to be bitten to be saved, then let them."

Cronin closed his eyes slowly and gave the smallest of nods.

Eiji snorted. "The next thousand years with you Alec are going to be so much fun."

Jodis put her hand up. "I'd also like to say a few words before we do this. Cronin, we will be with you, by your and Alec's side, forever. Jacques, it is an honor to fight beside you. And Eiji, my dearest love," she looked at him and gently touched the side of his face. "If you leave me again to go kill yourself in sunlight—if you put me through that or anything like it one more time—I will kill you myself."

Eiji grinned at her. "And my heart belongs to you too, my love."

Jacques gave a slow nod. "May the gods be looking upon us tonight."

Alec put his arms around Cronin, for a long embrace. "I have no regrets."

Cronin grabbed his face with both hands and kissed him hard. "*Beatha gun aithreachas.*"

Jodis smiled. "No regrets."

Eiji gave a nod. "No regrets."

Jacques joined in as well. "No regrets."

So this was it, Alec thought as he slid on his night vision goggles.

They each picked up a sledgehammer, stood in a close circle facing outwards, and with a deep breath from Cronin, they were gone.

———

THEY STOOD in what Alec remembered from the online pictures was the reception area were tourists gathered before going inside the first pit of Terracotta soldiers. Not one second later, Kennard and another four vampires arrived, armed and armored like them. Alec recognized one of them as Lars, the pyrokinetic guy from the bar in London.

Kennard, impish yet lethal, bowed his head in greeting. He looked at each of them and the hammers they were holding and smiled at Alec. "How very *Thor* of you."

"Thank you for coming," Alec said.

"Nice glasses," Kennard replied.

Alec automatically touched the night vision goggles. "Human eyesight's a bitch."

Just then, a wild braying sound cried out from inside the warehouse, and everyone turned to the sound. "They know you're here, Alec," Jodis said.

Alec took a step closer to Cronin. "Then let's not keep them waiting."

Eiji laughed and swung the sledgehammer. "Let's not."

"Strategies as discussed haven't changed?" Kennard asked, walking toward the doors with them.

"Not a thing," Cronin replied.

Alec held the hammer in his left hand, his pistol in his right. Jodis kicked the double entrance doors open, and they burst inside to a spectacular kind of hell.

THE HANGAR STYLE warehouse was exactly like all the internet pictures showed—roughly the size of a football field, with small wings off to each side—only this was in full-animated horror.

Like his blood spoke to them, Alec watched in morbid curiosity as the warehouse full of Terracotta Soldiers turned to face him. Some were still in the long pits, hopelessly trying to climb their way out. Some statues watched in horror as their hands crumbled against the dirt walls of the pits or their clay legs would snap as they tried to climb and step. Some had no heads at all, yet they still moved as though they knew where they wanted to go.

Other soldiers moved more fluidly, easier, yet still robotic and sluggish. They spoke in dusty rasps, words Alec couldn't make out, and they took mechanical and painful steps toward him. But most frightening were the horses. Alec could only see three of them, large and hulking. They looked like horses but were still somehow terribly deformed, as though the terracotta shell they wore hid a horrific mess inside. They made strangled braying noises that were more scream than sound. They reared their heads back, whinnying in pain.

Something wasn't right.

Alec had expected to come under attack, swinging blades, arrows, spears, something. But these statues were clumsy and unarmed.

"Well, this is disappointing," Kennard said.

Eiji laughed, but swung his sledgehammer at one soldier, sending it flying backwards in a spray of shards and dust.

"These are just mindless drones," Cronin said. "We need to move to the back. There must be something we're missing."

"Can you hear anything?" Alec asked him. "Feel anything?"

Cronin shook his head. "Nothing."

"Let's move to the back," Jodis said.

"We'll look in the side pits," Kennard said. He broke his team into two groups and sent them into pit two and pit three.

In the main pit, where a few hundred terracotta soldiers still fought to get out, there were long, raised dirt walkways which ran the length of the pit at head height of the soldiers still confined there.

Eiji ran first, with Jodis right on his heel, and leapt cleanly from the front of the warehouse onto the high dirt walkways. As the first of the terracotta soldiers tried to reach for their feet, Eiji swung his sledgehammer, decimating it to dust.

Alec and Cronin ran after them. Cronin made the jump easily whereas Alec, while he made the jump, didn't land with the grace the vampires did.

He clambered to his feet, just as a soldier grabbed at his leg. Cronin swung his sledgehammer at the soldier, knocking its head off like a football. The headless soldier stood still for a second, giving Alec enough time to get away from it, then it kept trying to grab at Alec.

"Keep running," Cronin told him.

Alec did. He took off along the narrow dirt catwalk and Cronin followed right after him. Eiji and Jodis were stopped near the end, where there were clay brick walls built in the pit and the majority of the soldiers couldn't reach them. There were a few select soldiers and horses, but Jodis took care of them on one side and Cronin took care of the other side.

Jacques, Kennard, and his English friends came from both sides, turning any soldiers into dust on their way back to where the others stood. "Pits two and three are empty," Kennard told them.

"Something's really wrong," Alec said.

"Is it a trap?" one of Kennard's men asked.

"Listen," Eiji said as he tapped the ground with his foot. "Can you hear that?" He tapped the dirt ground again and smiled.

Cronin answered. "It's hollow."

Without another word, Eiji, Jodis, and Cronin each lifted their sledgehammers above their heads and smashed them into the ground between their feet. And sure enough, a shell no thicker than a house brick fell away to reveal a secret entrance. As they removed more dirt, Alec realized he was looking at a set of stone steps leading down into the darkness. It reminded him of the small stairways in the underground tunnels beneath the Egyptian pyramids.... And it clicked. "This will lead us to the tomb of Emperor Qin," Alec said. "The Chinese pyramid. That's where we're supposed to go."

"What about Khan?" Jodis asked.

"Maybe he wants to bring back the First Emperor," Alec suggested. "Eleanor said she couldn't see."

"Our seer couldn't tell us either," Kennard admitted.

"And yet you came along anyway," Eiji said.

Kennard grinned at him. "Of course I did. Can't let you guys have all the fun."

"Yeah, it's all fun and games," Alec said with a snort, "until someone gets a stake to the heart."

Kennard laughed, and looking at Alec's sledgehammer, said, "May I?"

Alec handed it to him, and the small English coven leader took a few dainty steps along the dirt walkway and struck at two terracotta soldiers who were still trying to climb out of the pit. Alec laughed. "Oh, Happy Gilmore style." One of the English guys laughed, and Alec waved his hand at him. "Oh, finally! Someone who gets my movie references!"

Cronin chuckled and attention turned back to the new hole they'd made in the walkway. Jodis looked at the descending stairs. "Well, shall we?"

Jacques volunteered to go first, then Eiji and Jodis jumped down. Cronin went in with Alec, followed by Kennard and his team.

The dirt stairs were no more than three feet wide and went down maybe fifteen feet and opened out into a wider corridor. It was dirt and looked old and cut out of the earth by hand, and if it weren't for Alec's night vision goggles, he wouldn't have been able to see his hand in front of his face.

"We're headed west," Jacques noted as they walked forward.

"Toward the tomb," Alec said. "Yes. The tomb lay about a mile west of the Terracotta Army."

"Stop," Eiji put his hand up. "Listen."

In the eerie quiet, Alec could hear it too. "Footsteps in dirt," he said. "Slow and shuffling."

"You can hear that?" Kennard whispered.

"He has taken on some vampire abilities," Cronin answered curtly. "We don't know why."

Alec turned to Cronin. "Can you hear anything? Can you *see* anything?"

"No," he replied. "Only the talents of those around us, nothing else."

"What?" Kennard hissed. "What do you mean you can't see?"

"No, see the talent of others, or sense them at least," Alec answered. "My blood gives him transfer properties when he drinks it."

"Well, aren't you two just a wonderful web of weird," Kennard said flatly.

Just then, a small platoon of terracotta soldiers came out of the darkness. They moved in synchronized formation and slowly and robotically came toward them.

"And you didn't consider *not* drinking his blood, Cronin?" Kennard asked.

"It was a deliberate decision," Cronin answered. He took a more comfortable grip on the sledgehammer and never took his eyes off the approaching soldiers. "If I can transfer or even detect the talents of Khan or those around him, then it will give us a clear advantage."

Jacques and Eiji stepped forward and swung at the terracotta soldiers. They weren't armed, but they moved better and seemed to have some mental capacity compared to the ones they'd encountered in the main warehouse pit. It only took eight swings of hammers and they were nothing but dust.

"A clear advantage indeed," Kennard said, stepping over the broken shards of soldiers as they walked. "Alec, I cannot wait to see what talents behold you, my friend. A transfer, I suspect."

"How about we just get through this first?" Alec said, dismissing the idea. "I have a feeling we're walking right to where he wants us."

Eiji looked back at Alec and gave a nod before crouching lower and walking a little faster.

The next platoon of terracotta soldiers moved faster again, with more strength and agility than the previous ones, and the platoon after that even more so. It was clear to Alec the weaker—maybe the soldiers created earlier—were sent out first.

But still, they were hardly any match for them. Glorious and imperial but useless in combat.

Cronin licked his lips and furrowed his brows. "Can anyone else taste that?"

"I thought I was imagining it," one of the Englishmen said.

Jodis nodded. "I can. It's not metallic. It's not chemical."

Eiji crouched down to a shattered terracotta soldier. He picked up a shard of broken clay, smelled it before he crumbled it to dust, and put it to his mouth to taste. He stared at Cronin. "It's gu. Baked into the terracotta."

Cronin hissed and ripped a shred of his shirt off. He handed it to Alec. "Put this to your mouth and nose. Now."

"What's gu?" Alec asked as he covered his mouth and nose with the scrunched up material.

"Ancient poison," Eiji said. "Made specifically by putting venomous animals like centipedes, snakes, scorpions in a closed vessel until only one remains. It will have eaten all the rest and ingested all the combined toxins—the toxin is then extracted from the surviving animal and used on weapons or in drink."

"Or baked into the Terracotta Army," Jodis said quietly. "A silent defense to those who would try and destroy them."

"Alec," Cronin whispered. He put his hand to Alec's cheek. "Are you well?"

"I feel fine," he said, when the truth was he wasn't sure how he felt. He was hot and it was hard to breathe, but he'd just basically run half a mile carrying a sledgehammer, he was wearing night vision goggles and a backpack, and the air in the tunnel wasn't exactly fresh. "I'm fine."

"Are you certain?" Cronin pressed.

Alec nodded and put the ripped cloth to his face. "Let's keep going."

Cronin's eyes hardened but he didn't say anything. Alec took his hand, and they kept on their way. The platoons kept coming faster, one after the other, and Cronin kept Alec at the rear to be as far away from the poisonous dust as possible. Jacques and Eiji swung hammers into them and the English took care of others with their stakes. Jodis hung back like a personal guard to Cronin and Alec.

When the next wave of Terracotta Soldiers was decimated and they'd gone over half a mile, Cronin stopped walking. Alec pulled on Cronin's hand to keep him moving forward. But he stayed still. His grip on Alec's hand tightened and his eyes were unfocused.

"What is it?"

"Something's not clear," he said cryptically. "I can see something, but it's obscured from view."

"What do you mean you can see something?" Jodis asked. "In your head?"

Cronin nodded. "Another vampire is close."

"And you can see in their head?" Kennard whispered.

"I can see their talent. They're a cloaker."

"Shit." Alec knew from what they'd told him that cloakers were dangerous. They could hide events or other vampires, depending on their exact talent. "Can you see what they're hiding?"

Cronin shook his head quickly. "Imagine a room with windows, you can see out of all them but one is opaque and obscured."

"Okay then," Alec conceded. "Can you feel their talent?"

Cronin closed his eyes. "I think so. I'm not sure. It's very strange."

"Can you use it to cloak us?" Alec asked.

Cronin opened his eyes and shook his head. "No. I wouldn't know how."

"Or our plans, at least," Alec continued.

"We don't have any plans, Alec," Eiji said flatly. "I seem to recall your grand plan was to leap here with a sledge-hammer and smash shit up."

Kennard laughed and Alec shrugged at him. "And that's worked pretty good so far." Alec squeezed Cronin's hand. "Keep trying, I know you can do this. But we have to keep moving forward." He put the cloth to his face and looked down the tunnel.

Again, Jacques and Eiji went first and the English were next, but the next platoon of soldiers were faster and more agile. And armed. Jodis joined in the fighting, and when more soldiers kept coming, Cronin and Alec did too.

Alec swung his sledgehammer at the stomach of the closest clay soldier. The metal hammer busted a hole in its side and terracotta fell away in shards, yet the soldier kept coming. It had a wooden sword and swung it at Alec, just as Cronin put a sledgehammer through its heart and it fell. Alec staggered back a step, collecting himself against the tunnel wall. "Thank you."

"You're most welcome," Cronin replied with a slight bow.

When that battalion of soldiers was done, without a word of how close that one was or how much more adept at fighting the terracotta army were getting, they kept going west in the tunnel.

Alec was feeling it now. Was the air thicker or were his lungs not expanding properly? This is what Eleanor had meant. She said the air was thick, and now Alec knew why. Thick with poisonous dust. Dust that didn't affect vampires but was sure as hell harmful to humans. His lungs were squeezing and he felt hot, *too* hot. It made the pace he was keeping impossible and he almost tripped.

"Alec!" Cronin cried. Everyone stopped and turned to face him.

Alec leaned over and put his hands on his knees, trying to catch his breath. "I'm alright."

"You're not alright," Cronin said. "Where's the cloth for your face?"

"I must have dropped it," Alec said, aware of the wheezing sound he was making on each inhale.

"Here," Cronin said, pulling at his shirt. "I'll make you another."

Alec put his hand out to stop him and shook his head. "I don't think it matters at this point."

Eiji walked from the front of the group to the back. He put his hand on Alec's shoulder. "Alec," he whispered. "What are you saying?"

Alec wouldn't say he wasn't well or that he felt like he was trying to breathe through sand. He looked at Cronin and held out his hand; each breath was becoming rough and labored. "We need to hurry."

Of course, running was almost impossible and Alec was falling farther and farther behind with each step. "I will carry you," Cronin said, his voice ripped with anguish.

Alec shook his head. "No. We'll walk in there together, huh?"

"Alec," Cronin shook his head. His eyes were full of tears, his hands were trembling. "Tell me what to do?"

Before Alec could answer, they were set upon by another platoon of terracotta soldiers. They moved like normal vampires and were armed with shaolin sticks and were evidently trained in hand-to-hand combat. Alec stayed back, not wanting to be a liability. But there were many of them, and Cronin dropped the sledgehammer, opting for a wooden stake in each hand. And in the blink of an eye, he leapt a dozen times, spearing soldier after soldier in the heart like a violent strobe light.

When he'd killed them all, Eiji mumbled, "Show off."

One of the Englishmen, the leaper that brought them here, grinned with wide eyes. "You must teach me how to do that."

Cronin ignored them both and rushed back to Alec, putting his arm around him and helping him stand up straight. Alec tried to take quieter, more calculated breaths, but considering he was in the company of vampires with impeccable hearing, it was pointless.

"Come on," Cronin barked at the whole group. "Let's go. He's running out of time."

They moved forward again but a few yards later encountered another wave of soldiers. Alec leaned against the wall and took out his pistol. He raised his arm into the firing position and concentrated on his breathing. This battalion of soldiers must have been bigger because it took longer, and the pistol felt like it weighed a ton. When he dropped his hand, unable to hold it up any longer, Jacques and Jodis quickly stood in front of him, guarding him. Cronin, Eiji, Kennard, and the others took care of the soldiers, and when they were done, the air was thick with dust.

Cronin put his arm around Alec's shoulder, and Jodis did the same on the other side, helping him walk.

Alec was dizzy now, hot and sweaty, and his breaths were short and hard. And just when Alec was sure he couldn't take another step, Eiji stopped and put his hand up. "Ahead, fifty yards."

"The air is different," Cronin whispered. "Cleaner. Come on."

Alec's feet barely touched the ground as Cronin and Jodis ran into an cavernous arena. In his fuzzy mind, he could barely take in the space they'd walked into. If the Terracotta Army hangar was big, this was huge. Maybe four football fields in size, it was an underground city. No, Alec realized, a model of a Chinese city with stone gardens and small buildings that reminded Alec of stone box coffins. The center focus was an altar. Behind that was a mausoleum, huge and over compensating, stone and encased with gold and jewels, complete with a thousand-strong Terracotta Army welcoming committee.

From everything Alec had read and researched on this, which admittedly wasn't much, Alec knew where he was. He was under Mount Li, in the tomb of the First Emperor of China. He was the one who ordered the Terracotta Army be built. He was their creator, and they now lined either side of a path in their hundreds. A path, Alec knew, they were to walk. Outnumbered a hundred to one, they had no choice.

"Say the word and I will leap us all out of here," Cronin whispered.

Alec shook his head. He wheezed, "No. Let's see this done."

The Terracotta Army stood still and silent. Alec imagined they were proud to stand united. They turned in unison to stare at him, drawn by his blood, and the soldiers that lined the path leaned their shaolin sticks toward the center mausoleum, pointing the way they were to walk.

Without another word between them, they started to walk down the path. Now Jacques led them, followed by the English vampires, then Kennard. Cronin all but carried Alec, and Jodis and Eiji had their backs.

"Jorge is here," Cronin whispered. "Five vampires. One cloaker, one mason, one leaper, one bodyguard, and Genghis. Genghis is a manipulator. Alec you were right. He influences."

As they walked up the path, the soldiers filed in formation behind them, blocking the path. There was no going back. Ahead of them, at the end of the path, were stone steps leading up to a platform before the mausoleum.

And there waiting to greet them was Genghis Khan.

CHAPTER FIFTEEN

ALEC LAUGHED. Though it hurt his lungs and his head, he couldn't help it. Genghis Khan had a foreboding reputation as a ruthless conqueror, a man that claimed half the world, taken with brutal force and damnation, so Alec was expecting a little more.

"Alec?" Cronin questioned. "What is it?"

Alec snorted, which became a coughing fit, and Cronin stopped walking to let him settle. When the coughing subsided, Alec gripped his side, where a stabbing pain jabbed at what Alec was pretty sure was his liver. "Oh, nothing," he said breathily. "Just didn't think *the* Genghis Khan would look like Mr. Miyagi."

He was, Alec supposed, somewhat accurately described by historians. Given they didn't exactly have photographs in the thirteenth century, so paintings and drawings of the ruler weren't exactly gospel. Unless he sanctioned the artists to draw himself taller, Alec wasn't sure, but the guy was short.

Dressed in white and brown robes with a weird little gray goatee, he extended both arms in welcome, as though they were all long-awaited friends, and bellowed out words Alec could not understand. "He says welcome," Cronin translated. "He knew the key would come."

Eiji bowed but did not take his eyes off Genghis, then proceeded to speak in not-English. Alec was too tired to keep up with it. His body hurt, his brain, his lungs, and his legs were too heavy to lift. Cronin explained what was said. "Eiji said if he welcomed us so warmly and wished for our company, why send soldiers to kill us. Why harm the key?"

Genghis laughed and Cronin translated what he said. "I wanted the key here, but I also wanted to make sure he couldn't leave."

Then Genghis broke out in some convoluted soliloquy that Cronin translated in parts. "He needs the blood of the key to resurrect Qin, the First Emperor. He believes his mighty ancestor will bestow him great honor and power. And immortality, of course."

Alec knew the ancient Chinese religion believed in Earth, Sky, and Ancestors, and he felt stupid for not seeing the connection to the Emperor sooner. "What about the other elements?" Alec said. The words hurt as he spoke. "Doesn't he need all five?"

Cronin shook his head. "He seems to believe he just needs you, just the key. The fifth is the center of them all. The key is all he needs."

Alec stood up straight as much as it hurt. He stared at Genghis. "The key is no use to you when he's dead."

Genghis clearly had no clue what he said. He just smiled and extended one arm, as if inviting them all up the steps onto the platform. So apparently all conversations were going to be in Chinese or Mongolian—Alec had no clue—and he couldn't bring himself to care. He was sick. No, not just sick. He was dying. He was sure of it. His muscles were starting to cramp, he was now sweating like he'd run a marathon, and a dozen knives of fire twisted in his lungs with every breath. He tasted bile in his throat.

He wanted to sit down. If he could just lay down a minute....

Still with only one arm around Alec's shoulder, Cronin carried him up the steps and kept him on his feet. Everything was kind of hazy, like the focus on a camera zooming in and out, but Alec was sure the stone platform was a circle. There were other vampires there, sitting down, Alec realized. They were sitting on stone pews that formed a smaller circle, and then inside that was a sundial? No, Alec thought. Not a sundial, the stone plate Eleanor told them about.

Then he noticed Jorge.

The little vampire child was huddled, holding his knees to his chest with his back against the stone tomb. Not in the inner circle, but cast off to the side. He was the bait that lured them all there, because Genghis knew they'd come for him. Jorge's eyeballs were entirely black again, his little-boy fangs peeked out from his lips, and there was no mistaking the tears that ran down his cheeks. The little boy was crying.

A large male vampire stood over him, who Alec realized was a bodyguard holding him hostage.

Alec ignored the not-English ranting of Genghis Khan and looked at Jorge. "You okay?" he asked him.

Jorge shook his head. "Jorge wants to go home."

Yep, Alec thought. You're not alone there, kiddo. It took a second for Alec's hazy mind to think of the name of the man who looks after Jorge. "Where's Adelmo?"

Fresh tears fell from his eyes. "Jorge wants to go home."

"Me too."

"The key is dying," Jorge sobbed. "Silver river, silver river." Alec nodded and started coughing—it felt like he had lava in his lungs—and his whole body hurt. "Our mind sees what our eyes cannot. Jorge's mind sees. Silver river. Blood and stone."

Oh, great, Alec thought. He's still stuck on that blood and stone bullshit. Alec could barely remember his own name right then, his whole brain felt like it was on fire, let alone even try to decipher Jorge's cryptic riddles.

"The earth belongs to the silver river. Look with your mind like Jorge's does," Jorge said, and the tall vampire sneered, pulled back his hand, and struck Jorge across the face to shut him up.

Everyone reacted immediately, crouching and growling. Cronin tightened his hold on Alec, but Eiji drew two wooden stakes from his thigh holster and aimed them at the man who hit Jorge. "Touch the child again and it will be the last thing you do."

The man sneered at Eiji, but Genghis raised his hand putting an end to any discussions that didn't involve him.

The earth belongs to the silver river.

Alec's mind swirled as slow as quicksand in a dozen different ways. A sludge so thick and acidic, he couldn't make sense of any of it.

And everyone was talking in languages he couldn't understand, the noise was coming in ebbs and flows, tidal swells of consciousness. He could feel Cronin's arms around him, keeping him up, holding him. His soft voice, melodic in his ear, Scottish brogue he couldn't understand, but that sound—that perfect sound—kept Alec's eyes open.

Then he was being laid down on one of the stone pews. Alec knew his friends were around him, standing, protecting him. He knew Cronin still held his hand, still spoke in lilting hues of angels.

Look with your mind. Like Jorge does.

Then the voices were arguing, so many voices. Eiji and Jacques, Kennard, all of them arguing with Genghis, and the noise was becoming overwhelming. He tried to block them out, tried to concentrate on Cronin's words, his touch, and as he lay there with his head turned, he could see Jorge crying and mumbling to himself, or was he speaking out loud, or just in Alec's head? Alec wasn't sure.

Then, somehow, he remembered the watch. Fumbling with leaden hands, Alec reached into his jeans pocket and pulled out the watch that he'd given Jorge, that they'd taken from him to lure them all here.

Jorge's eyes widened when he saw what Alec was holding, and he started to smile. He quickly scampered across the floor, through the pillars of legs, and grabbed Alec's hand, taking the watch before the tall vampire pulled him back.

He thought he heard Cronin gasp, but everything swirled, he was so hot—too hot—and Alec knew this wasn't going to plan.

He knew his breaths were sharp and short. And numbered. He was burning from the inside out, the poison was leaching into every part of him. He had to tell Cronin one last thing. He had to tell him. He gripped Cronin's hand and tried to speak. But he couldn't get the air in his lungs to work.

The pain and weight was too much, and he closed his eyes, needing every ounce of energy so he could say these last words. Cronin leaned in real close. "Alec? What is it?" It sounded like a tortured sob. His voice was burdened with the pain Alec felt.

"Don't," Alec rasped. "Don't you dare... don't you dare let me die."

Alec could rest then, he thought, just for a moment. A tormented growl cracked through the air, and Alec didn't hear any of the mayhem after that.

CRONIN SAW it as soon as Jorge's hand touched Alec's. He knew what it was immediately: a transference of vision. He was holding Alec's hand when Jorge touched him, using Alec as a conductor between them, allowing Cronin to see into Jorge's mind. The briefest of moments, he saw it.

Look with your mind. Like Jorge does.

It wasn't a jumbled mess like he would have assumed, it wasn't split into different versions of Jorge. It was crystal clear.

He wondered if he could use the cloaker's powers to shield his friends, to protect them, or if he could use Genghis' powers of persuasion against him. Cronin thought, for just one second, about delving into the madman's mind.

And then he thought of a much quicker way.

Cronin pulled the pistol from Alec's holster and without another word, he shot Genghis Khan in the heart, then the tall vampire who guarded Jorge. Both men crumbled to dust, and Jorge ran through the vampires to stand, hiding behind Cronin. Eiji, Jodis, and Jacques reacted immediately, arming themselves and crouching into defensive positions.

"Cronin?" Eiji asked, not taking his eyes off the two remaining vampires. "What's going on?"

"It really was much quicker," he replied. "Alec was right. It was never Genghis Khan. He was no more than a ruse." Cronin turned to look at the Terracotta soldiers. "Look at them. They haven't moved. Khan never controlled them like he thought he did. He was no more than a puppet."

"How do you know?" Jodis asked.

"Jorge showed me in his mind. He saw him."

"Saw who?" Kennard asked.

"Who's been behind this the whole time," Cronin said. "Alec was right all along." Cronin simply aimed the handgun at two of the other vampires, who were suddenly very outnumbered. "Where is he?"

A burst of laughter came from nowhere, then a vampire, shrouded with a dark hood, literally seemed to appear from thin air. His face was obscured by the hood but Jacques reacted immediately. He stood in front of Cronin and Alec, facing this new enemy with a stake in each hand. "He is the one who killed Mikka, the one Alec chased through the alleys of New York City."

The man laughed again and lowered his hood. He had olive skin and short black hair and a sinister smile. "My name is Rilind. I am the sole remaining Autariatae, and I am here to reclaim what is mine."

Cronin could not hide his shock. This man was Illyrian. Ancient Illyrian, the sole survivor from a coven that was eradicated, or so he thought. The Autariatae were known for their cruelty and savagery, even against their own people. "How is it so?"

Rilind grinned at him, clearly pleased to have an audience. "I have certain skills. One in particular Cronin will not allow me killed for, isn't that right?"

Cronin growled low at him. "How do you know my name?"

Rilind laughed, the sound echoing menacingly in the

underground catacomb. "I know everything." He looked pitifully upon Alec. "Listen to his heart, so labored and slow. His breaths are like last season's fallen leaves when I walk upon them. So sad for you to watch him die."

A symphony of hisses and growls snapped through the air, but Rilind only smiled further. "As I watched my people die, you will watch yours. This key for all mankind will serve no one but me." He sneered at Cronin. "You Celts should have stayed in your caves, Cronin, all those years ago. And believe me, when I'm done, you'll wish you had."

"Tell me why I shouldn't kill you now?" Eiji asked, his tone was low and threatening.

"As my name suggests, Rilind is Illyrian for rebirth and regeneration. I am the only one who can bring the key back to life," Rilind answered. "Long enough to make him mine anyway."

Cronin snapped out a growl and bared his teeth. His whole body shook with rage. "He'll *never* belong to you."

"When you are dust and only he and I remain, he will belong to me. His power will be mine," Rilind said calmly. "Or should I let you live a thousand years of hell, as I have done, so you may know how it feels?" The two other vampires moved to stand on either side of Rilind.

Cronin concentrated on the other two for a second and told the others, "The woman is a mason, the man a cloaker."

Rilind quirked an eyebrow but his smile never faltered. "Does the leaper hide unbidden talents?"

"The *leaper*," Cronin sneered at him, "is tired of games." Just then, Cronin felt a small hand on the back of his leg, Jorge's hand. And his mind flashed with images of a dozen other vampires behind Rilind, all unseen, wearing cloaks, all standing still and silent.

Cronin raised the pistol and shot the man beside

Rilind, the cloaker. And no sooner had the vampire fallen to dust on the ground, then twelve other vampires appeared—the cloak that hid them, disappearing with their maker.

Rilind looked smug. "Be careful with your aim, Cronin. If I die, so does Ailig."

"Do not call him by name," Cronin hissed at him.

Rilind laughed. "I am the only one who can give him life."

"You knew he would be born?" Eiji asked, though it really wasn't a question.

"Of course I knew," Rilind scoffed. "I am from the Autariatae people. I was human almost a thousand years before you, young Eiji. We were mighty in power until the Celts took what was ours." He scowled at Cronin. "My maker was more druid than vampire. He told me of my own power, how it would be unsurpassed until a human key would be born, fated to a Celt, no less. Told me when, where, everything. It was unfortunate I had to kill him before he told anyone else. I rather liked him."

The twelve vampires moved in formation behind Rilind, silent and autonomous, and the tables of favor and numbers were turned once again. Cronin was barreled with an array of different talents, all pertaining to different levels of the elements: water, fire, earth, and air.

"You created Queen Keket," Jodis accused Rilind.

"And Genghis Khan," Rilind added. "Both fools for power that would never be theirs."

"Why?" Kennard asked.

"It makes sense to take out two of the biggest covens before I announce my return, don't you think? Anyway, the Egyptians got what they deserved," Rilind answered. "They killed my coven, as did Genghis. And what little remained of us was made obsolete by your elders after the Black Plague had their fun."

"Fun?" Cronin spat.

"What is it to live two millennia without a little sport?"

"The life of my Alec is not a game!" Cronin roared. "Enough of this time wasting. Tell us what it is you require of him so he may live!"

Rilind smiled, slow and spreading. "I thought you may never ask." He waved his hand at the stone mausoleum behind him. It was large, some forty feet across, and resembled the brickwork of the Great Wall. "The ancient Chinese thought their first Emperor was the missing element, but they were wrong. Your human is the missing element, the one who completes my little game. Well, his blood does."

"His blood is killing him," Cronin bit back.

"And yet, it will give him eternal life when I save him," Rilind said, tilting his head. "Or, he'll die. Either way, it won't matter to me." He smiled again. "There are ancient forces at play here, Cronin. Forces so powerful not even our vampire ancestors could fathom it. The Egyptians and the Chinese were fools to think they could bear it."

Alec took in a ragged breath. His lungs sounded like they were liquefying, his heart was barely beating, and Cronin couldn't take it anymore. "You speak of our vampire ancestors, of forces from long ago. If you will grant me but a moment, I will tell you what I know of men born of this day, like Alec," Cronin said, his voice was eerily serene despite the turmoil and pain he felt inside. "He would often say *we* speak like poetry and have a quiet grace that only patience and time can allow." Cronin smiled then. "He also has a saying, true from his time, you might find cementing in fortitude."

Rilind tilted his head again, amused. "And what is that?"

Cronin took a deep breath and concentrated on the woman mason across from him. He transferred her talent with just his mind, and smiled. "Alec would say 'Fuck this shit.'" And with that, Cronin threw out his hands and cast all the power he could muster against the vampires that faced him.

CHAPTER SIXTEEN

LIKE A HOLOCAUST FALLOUT, a wave of pure energy exploded outwards, turning the fourteen vampires facing them into stone—a coven of gargoyles sculpted in granite, faces frozen in shock and disbelief.

Eiji and Jodis turned to look at Cronin first, their eyes wide and mouths open. Kennard, equally astounded, scoffed out a laugh. "Cronin! You said fuck and shit!"

"Alec's worn off on me," Cronin mumbled, still staring at the statues in front of him. *Oh, Alec.* Cronin knelt quickly by Alec's side and took his hand. His skin was cool and clammy, his breaths forced and rattled, his heartbeat was weak. "We need to fix him."

"How?" Jodis cried. She knelt at Alec's other side and took his hand. "Alec, can you hear me. Alec, listen to me, sweet, sweet man. We're going to right this. I promise you."

"Rilind had the power of regeneration," Eiji said. "We could bring him back to life and make him heal him."

Cronin looked at Rilind's startled stone expression and shook his head. "No. Jorge, you said the red hand would hold him and he'd have forever. What did you mean?"

The little boy stared at Alec, and with the gentlest of touch, ran his finger down Alec's cheek. "Jorge is sad."

"Yes, I know," Cronin barked. "Jorge, he will die if we don't hurry. The red hand? And forever in the stones. Blood and stone. What does it mean?"

"Come, come," Jorge said. "The silver river." The little boy raced to the end of the circle platform and beckoned them with his hand. "Come, come."

Cronin scooped Alec up and carried him like a child. He was without resistance and slumped in his arms. He murmured a word, with barely a rattled breath. "Cronin."

"We're going to fix you," he replied, holding him a little tighter. "I swear it."

Jorge grabbed the stone plate and leapt from the platform and rounded the corner of the mausoleum. Fronted by sprawling steps reminiscent of Roman architecture, Jorge raced up to the huge doors.

"Wait!" Jacques called after him. "Stop!" Jorge did, thankfully, stop at the doors. "It's well documented this is booby-trapped with arrows and spears to fire upon anyone who enters."

The sound of stone scraping on dirt made them all turn. The Terracotta Army were moving, coming for them. *This* was their master, not Genghis Khan or Rilind who influenced them. This was their true master, and they would defend him of their own volition. They moved faster than the docile soldiers in the tunnel. These were the best of his army, and they were coming in fast. Cronin ran up to the wall beside the entrance. "Open the doors!"

Eiji and Jacques kicked in the doors and quickly stood with their backs to the wall, grabbing Jorge and pulling him to safety before a slew of arrows shot out the doors. But it wasn't the wooden arrows or stakes that concerned Cronin or the quickly approaching Terracotta Army. It was the cloying scent of what was in that tomb.

Not rotting flesh—the body of Qin was long ago mummified—it wasn't the stale air. It was the smell of mercury. A lot of it. *Rivers* of it. Silver rivers, as Jorge had called it.

Mercury wasn't harmful to vampires, yet from levels of the liquid metal never seen before, the fumes alone would turn Alec's brain to mush, his organs would shut down, his bone marrow and blood would turn to soup.

Jacques and the English vampires started staking the first of the soldiers who came at them, but there were too many of them. They started to swarm in, and Cronin knew he had no choice. He pulled Alec against him and ran inside. When all of them were in, Eiji and Jodis pulled the doors shut, and they turned around to see what they faced next.

It was a huge crypt, fifty feet squared, with a stone altar in the middle and a mummified body presented atop it. It was surrounded by jars and furniture, weapons, statues and ornaments of jade, gold, and jewels glistened on almost every surface. But most beautiful and lethal were the rivers of flowing mercury. Untouched by millennia, slow and undulating, the silver metal flowed like water. Mapped the same as the watercourses of China, this remarkable tributary replica was the reason no human would open the tomb: the mercury levels were off the charts.

"Here," Jorge said, still holding the stone plate, it was almost half his size. He was seemingly oblivious to everything in the tomb. *Maybe he'd seen it in his head before,* Cronin thought, *so he was not shocked by what he saw now.* "Jorge take you."

Cronin followed Jorge as he ran, leaping over the

streams of quicksilver toward the altar. It was only when he was almost upon it, that Cronin could see a circle of stone around the final resting place of Qin, China's First Emperor.

"The four ancient elements," Jodis whispered, and she was right. There were four points around the circle: wood, water, metal, and fire.

The soldiers banging got louder and the wooden doors creaked in protest. They were really running out of time. "Jorge?" Cronin yelled. "What does it mean?"

The little boy's eyes were all black again and he rocked back and forth. "Blue moon. Silver river."

Jacques took the stone plate from the boy, and he ran to the closest river of mercury. He submerged it into the silver liquid. "The Ancient Chinese elements are on this stone," he said. He ran back to Cronin and put the stone plate on Alec's body. "The other elements. Collect them!"

Eiji lifted a wood stake from his thigh holster, and Jodis brought her hands together and with a great effort, formed a ball of ice in her hands and placed it carefully on the mercury-covered plate. Lars snapped his fingers and a small flame appeared. He collected an ancient coin, set it alight, and put it on the plate. Then Jacques took a blood bag from his backpack and, slicing it with his fingernail, poured Alec's blood onto the plate. "The key's blood in the center of the plate, all elements are brought together."

They each held their collective breaths and waited for a miracle to happen.

Nothing.

Nothing happened, at all.

Alec sucked back a ragged breath and choked and coughed on the exhale.

Cronin roared. "Jorge! It's not working!"

The boy shook his head and his eyes were clear. He spoke quietly and clearly. "Inside the stones. Not these stones but from where he came. From where his blood was born."

Cronin roared again and his whole body vibrated with anger. "Alec is dying in my arms, and all you have is cryptic riddles!"

"No!" Jorge stood and yelled back at him with more fire and rage Cronin would have given the boy credit for. "Look into Jorge's mind! See it! See it!"

Inside the stones, from where he came. From where his blood was born. Cronin closed his eyes and concentrated on Jorge's thoughts, and he saw exactly what Jorge saw. Cronin's eyes flew open just as the wooden door smashed inwards and the Terracotta Army flooded in. "Hold on to me!"

Everyone reached out and touched. Jodis picked up Jorge just as Eiji grabbed her arm, as the first of the soldier's arrows slung through the air, and Cronin leapt.

THE AIR WAS SO fresh and cold compared to the rank and humid catacomb in China, Alec convulsed in Cronin's arms. "It's almost time," Cronin whispered, holding him tighter still. "Just hold on for a few minutes more, m'cridhe."

"Why are we here?" Kennard asked, as they all looked around. It was almost sunrise, the sky was showing off hints of light and glory, and they were surrounded by standing stones.

"From where he came. From where Alec's blood was born, Jorge said," Cronin answered. "His father's family is from

Calanais. And these are the Calanais Stones, or Callanish Standing Stones, if you will. I would hazard to guess this is where the incubus in Alec's bloodline is from also." Jodis put Jorge on his feet and the boy beamed a smile that told Cronin he was right. Though he knew he was. He felt it in his bones.

The Callanish Stones stuck out of the earth like broken teeth. Glorious and ancient, Scotland's very own Stonehenge. A standing circle of fifteen stones, ancient, *so ancient*. Their meaning, their purpose, had been speculated about for thousands of years. And now Cronin knew. This is what they were for.

In the center of the circle was a shallow pit, dug into the earth thousands of years ago and Cronin lay Alec in it.

"Cronin," Jodis hissed. "Cronin!"

He looked up to find little Jorge standing with his arms out, his eyes pure black standing in the middle of the circle. But he was smiling, like a light was shining from his very being, beautiful and peaceful.

"Cronin," his voices said in unison. "Only you can do this."

Cronin could see into his mind, but it wasn't Jorge talking. It was a woman. She was in her twenties, with brown hair and green eyes. "Who are you?" he asked.

"I am Ailig's mother," the woman said. Her voice, coming from Jorge was like music, lyrical bells. "You must save him."

"Tell me how!" Cronin begged. "I cannot change him!" He looked to the east, where the sun was threatening to rise. "I am almost out of time."

"Stone, blood, metal, fire, and water, along with the moon and the sun," his mother answered, motioning toward the stone plate on Alec's chest. It was covered in mercury, fire, water, and the most important element of all, Alec's blood. "The elements of life will save him."

Cronin was out of patience; fear and anger surged in the form of tears. "How?"

"You have been designed for this," Jorge answered. "You can displace atoms by quantum physics, can you not?"

Cronin nodded. "I'm a leaper."

"And with his blood in your veins, you can transfer the powers of others, yes?"

Cronin scrubbed at his face. "Yes, but I don't really know how."

Alec's mother smiled in Jorge's mind. The little boy swayed. "The stones hold the powers of life, they will do the work. You need to channel it, transfer it, *leap* it into him. This has been a thousand years in the making. On this blue moon; every thing is aligned. This is what you were designed for, Cronin."

Cronin looked up at the small child vampire, and then at the faces of his friends. "Tell me what I have to do."

"As the sun breaks and the moon is still in the sky, you will feel the power from the stones."

Cronin nodded quickly. "Okay."

Then Jorge said, "You will need to kill him first."

Cronin stared at him. "What?"

"You cannot change what is already changed, Cronin."

"What do you mean?" Jodis demanded of the boy. "Please, we are running out of time!"

"Vampire blood already runs in his veins, that is why he could not be changed," Alec's mother's voice said serenely. "You must kill the vampire in him so the human can live. One breath only, Cronin. Then bite him."

Cronin was about to object—he couldn't do this, he could never kill any part of Alec—but a tremendous hum came from the earth like it reverberated within him, and his hands began to shake.

"It is starting," Jorge said. A look of sorrow and worry crossed Alec's mothers beautiful features. "You must do this. The key must be changed today."

Cronin looked at his friends and lastly at Eiji and Jodis. "You must go. You can't be here when the sun rises."

Jodis took Eiji's hand. "We're not leaving you," she whispered. "Or Alec."

"We shall stay also," Kennard said. He gave a weak, scared smile. "Can't let a bloody Scot think I'm a coward, can I?"

The hum got louder and stronger, and Cronin sat in the earthen pit with Alec laying across him, the Chinese stone plate with the five elements on it lay on Alec's chest. Cronin kissed Alec's lips, as a tear ran from the corner of his eye to his temple. His breaths were so faint now, so rasped and grating. He was hot to the touch, burning, sweating, and his hazel eyes were glassy. He looked about to die.

Eiji and Jodis were suddenly in the pit with Cronin, on the other side of Alec, both whispering words of love and pleading.

"Stay with us, Alec."

"Hold on, sweet Alec."

Eiji held a wooden stake. "You shouldn't have to be the one to do this."

Cronin shook his head and breathed through the pain. The hum in his chest was almost unbearable. "It should only be me." He took the wooden stake, and he looked to Jodis and Eiji. "If this doesn't work and he lives no more, promise me you will do the same to me."

The sun sent rays of yellow upward toward the moon.

"Now, Cronin," Alec's mother urged through Jorge. She pleaded. "Now!"

Cronin kissed Alec once more and whispered, "For forever, my love." And he drove a wooden stake into his heart.

Alec lurched forward, arching his back. His eyes wide, his mouth opened in a silent scream. He reached blindly, finding Cronin's face, twitching and convulsing before he sucked back a deep breath.

And this was it.

One breath only.

Cronin held him like a prayer in his hands and sunk his teeth into his neck. Alec touched Cronin's face and gripped his hair as Cronin drank his blood. The warmth, the pure taste of energy and life itself ran down his throat. And the hum that echoed in his chest now shook his very core. Cronin closed his eyes and let his head fall back, blood ran from the corners of his mouth, but he didn't care. He focused on every atom, every molecule of energy, and sent it with every ounce of strength he had into Alec.

Alec convulsed in his arms again, this time his chest pushed forward, heaving, and Cronin could feel the hum vibrating through Alec.

Light, not sunlight, not moonlight, but a white light gathered from the Callanish Stones around them, connecting and growing until it had gone full circle and it spun to the center, to Alec. The light went through him, it came out of him, it roared and surged, and it took all of Cronin's vampire strength to hold him. The energy was almost supernova, the light blinding and pure.

And then it was gone.

In its place was shock and silence. No one breathed. No one blinked.

Cronin didn't dare to even hope.

Then Alec convulsed and sucked back an enormous breath, and Jorge jumped up and down, clapping his hands. His eyes were back to normal, the visions of Alec's mother were gone from his mind. Cronin saw nothing but the beautiful man in his arms.

Then, with what was like the voice of god to Cronin, Alec screamed.

WITH BARELY SECONDS TO SPARE, Cronin leapt everyone back to Japan. They arrived back at the house in a burst of action. Everyone backed away, still wide-eyed and in shock at what they'd just witnessed. Cronin cradled Alec like a child as he moaned and writhed in pain. He gently put him on the floor and touched his face, his chest, his hair. He took his hand. "You are not alone, m'cridhe. My heart, my everything. Alec, I am right here."

"What's happening?" Kole asked, standing pale and scared near the door. He was staring at the dark blood stain on Alec's chest. "Someone tell me what's going on with him!"

"It's the transformation," Eiji answered. "He's becoming a vampire."

Kole put his hand to his mouth and nodded as the first of his tears fell. It took him a long time to speak. "Will he be okay?"

Still holding Alec's hand, Cronin put his other hand to the side of Alec's face. "He will be."

Jodis put her icy hands on Alec to cool him down, Cronin realized, and Alec relaxed a little. He gripped

Cronin's hand, his fingers like claws, and his teeth were clenched.

Then Jorge knelt at Alec's feet. His voice was Jorge's, but Cronin knew the words were of Alec's mother. And it all made sense to him now: Jorge didn't have multiple personalities. He spoke with the dead. He spoke for the dead, and like now, they spoke through him. "He bears a power never seen before in our kind, as he was destined to. Not one power, but *all* powers. Unequalled and unimaginable, but he is fair and just, and he will protect and serve. Fate has chosen well."

Jorge spoke directly to Cronin. "But such powers do not come without perils. There will always be those who seek to control or conquer him, and it will be a great responsibility to protect him, but protect him you will."

Cronin nodded. "Of course."

Jorge put his little hand on Alec's leg. "Alec, you have the power to heal. Can you feel it?"

Alec arched his back and his hands were tight fists, despite holding Cronin's hand. Cronin could feel the change of strength in him. The power he gripped his hand with was not human. But if he had the power to heal, as his mother suggested through Jorge, then he didn't have to suffer through the transformation. "Find the power to heal and embrace it, Alec," Cronin whispered. "Please."

With a strangled cry of exertion, Alec pushed through whatever boundaries he fought against. The wound on his chest healed over, his veins protruded under his skin, his eyes went wide, and with a final cry, he slumped heavily back to the floor. He was quiet for what felt like forever; his hands were no longer clenched, his heart rate was completely normal, and the silence was deafening. Then Alec laughed. "Well, shit. That was an easier way to do it, and probably something I could have been told half an hour ago."

Eiji burst out laughing, as did Jodis, who covered her mouth with her hands as tears spilled down her cheeks. Cronin couldn't help it. He laughed, and tears of joy and relief sprung to his eyes, and he made the first mistake of throwing his arms around Alec.

CHAPTER SEVENTEEN

ALEC DIDN'T MEAN to throw Cronin. He didn't mean to pounce after him, and he didn't mean to stand up and pull Cronin to his feet by his shirt. His whole perception of strength and distance and physical restrictions were not what they used to be.

Nothing was as it used to be.

The world was clearer, with a complete new spectrum of colors, and his vision was in permanent panoramic view. He heard everything—everything—and tasted it all on his tongue. His brain catalogued what everything was in less than a nanosecond, and his mind—oh, his mind—was an open universe.

He looked at Eiji and Jodis, who were both grinning from ear to ear, then at Jacques and Kennard, Lars and the other English vampires—he knew who they were now, Leonard, Omar, and Kylie. He didn't know how he knew, he just knew—and little Jorge who grinned fantastically. Eleanor and his dad were there, *oh Dad*, but there was Cronin....

Cronin.

He was smiling, looking at his ripped shirt, brushing it down, where Alec had grabbed him a second ago. Was that just a second ago?

Cronin. His perfect skin and rusty ginger-colored hair looked even better through these new eyes. His scent, his magnetic pull was so much better, and Alec couldn't restrain himself. He took Cronin's face in both hands and kissed him.

Eiji laughed. "He hasn't changed one bit."

Cronin squirmed, pulling Alec's hands from his face with a laugh. "Ah, not so strong."

Alec put his hands to Cronin's face as gently as he could and kissed him again. "Sorry. Everything is so...."

"Different?"

"Better." He looked around the room again and saw his dad. His very human father. His father with a beating heart and blood in his veins. Yet, in his mind, he compartmentalized the difference between food source and family. He walked, which by the surprise on his dad's face and how his hair blew back in the breeze, Alec assumed he walked a little too fast. He very slowly, very carefully, put his arms around him. "Dad."

Kole started to cry. "Oh, Alec. I wasn't sure I'd ever see you again."

Then little Jorge stood beside them, and in a woman's voice, said, "Kole?"

Then everything happened very quickly. Kole stumbled backwards as Alec spun around and ripped out a growl that was so loud and threatening, he frightened himself. But he had to protect his father at all costs, and he bared his fangs—Jesus, he had fangs—and he threw out his hands, sending snaps of electricity and fire and rage from his fingers.

Jorge put his hands up and the woman's voice murmured, "Be calm."

And Alec felt calm, but it wasn't until Cronin was in front of him with their foreheads pressed together that he breathed deep enough to center himself. "You're okay, your father's okay, Alec."

"It was Heather's voice!" Kole whispered. Alec turned around to see that he must have pushed his father over, because Eleanor was helping him get to his feet.

Jorge smiled serenely at Kole. "Oh, Kole. Yes, it's me."

"What...?" Kole said, shaking his head. "How...?"

Jorge waved his little hand. "This gifted child, so misunderstood, is a pathway for the taken."

Kole shook his head, so unsure, so scared.

It was extraordinary to hear a woman's voice come from the child, but Alec could somehow see into Jorge's mind. And it was clear and crisp, the woman Alec saw was the woman from the photographs his father had kept. "Those in the afterworld of our kind have watched for this," she said through Jorge. "We had to ensure our bloodline, the gifted blood—half vampire, half human—became what he was destined to become."

"I can see you," Alec said, staring at Jorge. "In his mind. I can see you."

"Alec, Ailig, your father raised you so well," she reached out her hand. "You and I will talk often. But for now we must leave."

Jorge's eyes returned to normal and the little boy grinned. "You see what Jorge sees!"

Alec nodded and put his hands to his hair. His mind was fractured, splintered into a hundred directions at full speed: sights, smells, memories, new things like other people's thoughts, hearing music from God knows how far away, knowing he can control things like fire and water. Jesus. It was all too much. His throat hurt, his stomach burned, he had mud in his hair. He pulled a clump of mud out and looked at it questioningly. Then he noticed he had a red-black stain on his chest and a hole in his shirt and he stunk of mercury and, oh God, he hugged his father with a poisonous shirt.

"Alec, it's okay," Cronin's voice was calm and smooth, like an audible Xanax. That thought made him laugh. Wait, did Cronin say that or did he think it?

Alec shook his head and his eyes burned. He pulled at his hair again. "It's all too much. I have so much in my head," he showed Cronin his hands. "I had fire and lightning on my hands! Did you see that? And I have so much energy and power in my bones." His hands started to shake. "And I have a clawing feeling in my stomach and my throat and I—"

Cronin put his hand to Alec's face. "You need to feed. It will help clear your head."

"Afterwards, take him to New York," Jodis said. "Spend a few days alone together, uninterrupted, without pressure or influence."

Cronin nodded. "Yes. Good idea."

Eiji walked over to Alec and took his hand. Alec was barraged with lines of molecular DNA, and he knew he was seeing Eiji's ancestral history. He couldn't make sense of it yet, or decipher what any of it meant, but he knew he would learn. "We will give you a few days grace, but we will help you learn." Then Eiji grinned widely at him. *Take it easy on my brother the first time, yes? You'll hurt him.*

"In the very best of ways," Alec replied.

Eiji's eyes widened and he laughed. "You heard my

thoughts? Do me a favor. Never tell me what Jodis is thinking about me. Not even if I beg."

Jodis chuckled and she put her hand on Alec, something she'd done a hundred times before, and Alec reflected her own power against her. He didn't use his own ability to produce ice by touch, he rebounded hers and she pulled back her hand. "Sorry," he said quickly.

Jodis laughed. "Don't ever apologize. I do think we'll be cataloguing a lot of powers, yes?"

"Um, probably," Alec said. He was so distracted by every damn thing, and that clawing in his stomach was getting worse.

"Go let him feed," Jodis said. She smiled proudly at Cronin. "Oh, I have longed to say that to you."

Cronin laughed, put his arm around Alec, and they were gone.

LEAPING the first time as a vampire wasn't any less difficult than the first time as a human. It wasn't painful, well, not physically. It was just that Alec had an ocean of strength and powers he couldn't control, and leaping was one of them.

It was like two men trying to waltz as the lead.

After what was essentially a bumpy ride, they landed in a back alley in Mexico City. It was dark, the air was humid and wet, and there was an onslaught of new senses, new sounds, new smells. Not all of them pleasant.

"Are you okay?" Cronin asked him quietly. "You have the ability to leap as well?"

"I think so," Alec said with a shrug. "But I think I should let you drive, because I'm not very good at it."

Cronin snorted out a laugh. "Yes, you should probably let me *drive*, while you're still learning." He shook his head and looked at Alec in wonder. "You're even more handsome now. You were so incredible, you *are* so incredible. You completed your own transformation by will alone! And it would seem you have an unending well of talents—more powerful than any of our kind before. You're remarkable, Alec."

Alec swallowed, then swallowed again.

"Oh," Cronin said. "I apologize. You need to feed. The first time will come as a shock to you, Alec. You may not even like it to begin with. You might be repulsed with yourself—"

There were so many voices, noises, more voices, scents, and more and more voices—Cronin's included—and he couldn't concentrate. He was hungry. He wanted it. He closed his eyes and blocked out everything else. He focused his many-faceted mind on listening for just one thing: conversations in the alleys of drugs, rape, or murder.

He opened his eyes and grinned at Cronin. And he ran. With a force and speed that was liberating, he scaled the wall easily and raced a few blocks over rooftops in mere seconds and stopped on a dime. Cronin was right beside him, his fangs unhidden by his smile: a glorious sight, so perfect, and so *his*.

He wanted to kiss him, to fuck him and bite him. But his throat burned and he wouldn't be distracted. He focused again, only this time on the th-thump-thump of blood pumping through veins, and there was no stopping him.

Alec appeared in front of a man covered with gold chains and rings, who had a small kid by the shirt collar up against the wall, telling him he would deliver the package or die.

Alec grabbed the man's shoulder and threw him backwards. The man smashed into a concrete wall, and Alec could hear bones snap and internal organs pulverize before he slid to the ground, very, very dead.

"Oops."

Cronin burst out laughing, the small kid took off and two other gang men ran out to meet them with handguns pointed directly at their heads. Alec felt no fear. In fact, he'd never felt more alive. He smiled at them and they both recoiled instantly. Then Alec remembered his fangs.

"Oh." He looked at Cronin and pointed to his own mouth. "I'm gonna have to learn how to do that retract thing."

Again, Cronin laughed and set after the two men who had turned to run away. He grabbed them both by the necks, rendering them unconscious, and led Alec farther up the alley until they were completely concealed by night. He pushed one of the men to Alec.

Cronin tilted the man's head to the side and spoke softly. "Watch me." He slid his lips over the pulse point on the man's neck. "You will know where to bite." And with a quick flex of his teeth, he punctured the skin and was drinking.

Alec was growling. He couldn't help it. He licked his lips, wanting to taste, not only the free-flowing fresh blood, but Cronin's mouth, his lips, his tongue. Alec lifted the man to his lips, feeling the pulse and lifeblood just under the skin. He pulled back his lips, and with what he was sure was much less grace and finesse, he bit into his neck.

The taste was hot and metallic, tangy and sweet. It was luscious and it was everything, and he drank quickly, draining the piece of shit human in seconds. And Alec knew he would do anything to taste it again.

Cronin was staring at him, his black eyes were on fire, he licked his lips as though he could taste the blood Alec was drinking. Then he pushed Alec up against the wall behind him, kissing him and gripping him everywhere. It was frantic and intense, pure want and need.

Alec spun Cronin around so he was pressing him against the wall, and kissed him as hard as he could. Cronin seemed to enjoy Alec's newfound strength, moaning with every push and touch. Alec put his hands under Cronin's ass and lifted him, spreading his thighs so Alec's hips were pressed right against him. And fully clothed, they writhed and rutted against each other, kissing and tasting, growling and gripping until Cronin went rigid against him and came.

Alec could not only feel his own pleasure, but he could feel Cronin's too. It barreled through him, Cronin's orgasm and his own, and Alec pushed the pleasure out from himself, reflecting it back to Cronin again and again, both of them coming and coming until Alec couldn't stand up.

Before he fell to the ground, Cronin must have leapt them, because they landed on the bed in Cronin's New York City apartment.

Both men lay on their backs, gasping, growling, grinning. "What... what... was that?" Cronin asked.

"I um, I'm not sure. When Jodis touched me earlier, I reflected her power back to her. Well, I reflected your pleasure back to you, then back to me and then back to you." Alec shrugged. "Well, I think that's what I did."

Cronin laughed and held his hands up. "My hands are still shaking. They've not done that since I was human."

Alec snorted. "So, we're gonna have some fun with these new powers, yes?"

Cronin sighed and rolled over to face Alec. "How do you feel?"

Alec thought of everything he felt. "Amazing. Energized. Very *sexual*," he said, and Cronin laughed. "I feel jittery. Nervous, confident, happy, relieved. Overwhelmed."

Cronin kissed him softly. "I think you've taken to everything extremely well. Better than anyone I've seen."

"I have so much to learn, so much to get used to. It's very overwhelming."

"And I will teach you everything. Eiji, Jodis, and I will teach you all we know." Cronin stared at him, his eyes shone with wonder. *You are more remarkable than I can say.*

"I am remarkable because of what you make me," Alec answered.

Cronin's eyes widened. "You hear my mind?"

Alec reached in the depths of Cronin's mind, seeing flashes of different times and places, long ago and far away, like snippets of cinematic masterpieces. "I see everything."

Then Cronin must have remembered their times in bed, because Alec was bombarded with not just explicit visuals, but how it made Cronin feel.

"Oh, Jesus," Alec panted. He squinted his eyes shut. "I'm gonna need to learn how to block that out."

Cronin laughed. "Or not."

Alec rolled off the bed and went to snatch the lube from a bedside table, only to be left holding the entire now-broken drawer in his hand. His strength was bewildering to him, though Cronin burst out laughing. It was the freest sound Alec had heard from him yet. Alec plucked out the small bottle of lube and carefully threw it on the bed, then pounced on Cronin, and pinned his hands to the bed. Matched in physical strength, like Cronin had done so many times before, Alec ripped Cronin's clothes from his body, then his own.

Cronin laughed, but the sound became a moan when

Alec pushed Cronin's thighs apart with his own. "You belong to me now," Alec said, holding him down. His fangs were pulsing with want, his cock thick and aching. He smeared lube over his cock, giving himself a few strokes, and the new vampire sensations made him hiss. It was *so* much better....

Cronin's chest arched forward, his head pushed back, and he exposed his neck to Alec. "Make me yours, Alec. Take from me what you will."

Alec pushed against Cronin's hole with his cock and kissed him hard, making Cronin whine and plead. He was stronger than Cronin now, he held him tighter, and he maneuvered him like he weighed nothing. And from the sounds Cronin made, he clearly liked being manhandled.

"Have me, please, I beg of you," Cronin whispered. "Alec, please."

Alec sunk his cock into Cronin's ass in one hard push and sunk his teeth into his neck. Cronin was his, for every whim of pleasure, to do with what he wished.

As he was to Cronin.

It was a pleasure so divine, so raw, and so complete. He was inside him, in every possible way. He was so deep inside him, he tasted his blood on his tongue: a taste so delectable, so perfectly designed just for him.

Cronin gripped his arms, his back, and his ass, not having to restrain his strength anymore, and begged—he begged—Alec to fuck him harder.

So he did.

And then they made love, and then Cronin fucked Alec, and then they made love again, and Alec wasn't sure for how many days it lasted.

Whatever it was, however long, it was not enough.

They were lying on the bathroom floor, taking a

moment to catch their breaths. "I have some pretty special powers, apparently," Alec said with a laugh.

"I'll say."

Alec snorted but was serious for a moment. "I can feel it. An energy bubbling in my bones. I can't describe it, but I'm kind of scared by it."

Cronin frowned and squeezed his hand. "Don't be afraid, m'cridhe."

"*My heart*. I love how you call me your heart," Alec repeated.

"It is true."

"Oh, that reminds me." He touched the new scar on his chest. "You stabbed me in the heart. Is that something we need to talk about?"

Cronin laughed, long and loud. "How long are you going to remind me of that?"

"Forever."

Cronin hummed contentedly. "I'll be truly disappointed if you don't."

EPILOGUE

~SIX MONTHS LATER~

IT HAD TAKEN some getting used to, but Alec was getting the hang of his powers. There was no use hiding them from the world; word had spread quickly that the one who had stopped Queen Keket, Genghis Khan, and their master Rilind from their quests of destruction had been reborn a vampire.

The stories of his untold powers soon followed.

There had been no sign of ill-regard toward him, in fact quite the opposite. Most people, or vampires to be exact, came from around the world offering gifts and thanks.

From the beginning, Alec had insisted on a counsel to show he would use his powers responsibly, for the betterment of vampires and humans alike. Cronin, Eiji, and Jodis would always hold rank on this counsel, but a leader, or spokesperson, from every continent would join them for meetings to discuss and raise any questions or concerns they may have.

The vampire population as a whole were pleased to have a unified counsel, governing laws and holding accountable the most powerful vampire to have lived. And they were even more pleased that it was Alec's idea. Alec had no doubt a time would come when someone thought themselves good enough to stand against him, but for now there was peace. Beautiful and soul-soothing peace.

Except for the time Alec accidently set fire to Jodis' favorite sofa, or the time he zapped Eiji with electricity— even though it was Eiji's idea to see how funny it would be —and Alec put him through two walls. Yeah, it was funny. Until they saw Jodis and Cronin's faces, then it wasn't funny. Well, not while they were around anyway.

The first thing Alec learned to do was block the thoughts of others. Not only was it a huge violation of their privacy, but there was shit Alec just didn't want to see. Or hear. As if vampire hearing wasn't enough to get used to, but full visuals of half the population of New York City was enough to make Alec want to live in Antarctica for a while.

Alec would sometimes use it to talk to Cronin, though only with his consent. And while mind reading had its advantages, in that Alec could see the true intentions of the hundreds of vampires he met, it also meant he could hear the thoughts of the humans he fed from.

That only happened one time. The very second time he fed—a mental picture slide show of life and happier times— and within an hour of that child-murderer's body hitting the ground, Alec taught himself how to block thoughts.

The others believed it might not be possible for him to learn such things so quickly, but Alec just shrugged. He told Cronin, "It was like having a hundred tabs open on your computer and simply muting one while all the others were fully functioning."

And once Alec learned to see how his mind worked, then everything became a whole lot easier. Cronin had thought that meeting so many vampires too soon might have been confronting or overwhelming, given Alec's ability to read and transfer their own talents, but the opposite was true. It helped him understand his own powers. Just a few minutes after meeting them, he had a better understanding of how to control fire, wind, water, other people, reflecting, transferring, the list seemed endless.

And there *was* a list.

Jodis had started documenting and recording all the talents Alec encountered and accrued. The list was long, and in all likelihood, it would be never-ending. Jodis would get excited and quickly write down every new thing. Alec didn't mind though. In fact, he adored Jodis and Eiji. They were like a sister and brother to him now, and Alec would be eternally grateful for their help, their friendship, and for how much they loved Cronin.

Alec hadn't been apart from Cronin at all since he was changed. Not a minute. Which was what made this separation so hard.

There was no pain like there used to be when they were apart, but the yearning to be with him again was hollow and uneasy.

"How you holding up?" Eiji asked, now standing beside him.

"I'm okay," Alec answered quietly. He stood in their New York apartment, in his and Cronin's bedroom, in front of the single shelf along the end wall. Upon it was the ax and helmet Cronin had with him when his human life ended. And now next to those was the stone plate, still stained with his human blood and mercury, that he held when his human life ended.

Alec was yet too scared to touch it. His mental strength was easy to understand, but his physical strength was something he had to work on. He had crushed countless pens, a football, his laptop, faucets, and a vase he didn't dare ask the age of. So he admired the stone plate with his hands behind his back.

"He has so many trinkets from the last twelve hundred years," Alec said, referring to the wall of artifacts in the living room and the ones in his office. "He's done so many amazing things."

"Alec, you have the sun-disk of Ra, an ancient Egyptian God, and the stone plate from the First Emperor of China to start your collection. I think you're doing okay."

Alec snorted. "Sounds so bizarre, doesn't it?"

Eiji studied him for a moment. "What is the real reason for this melancholy? Not having second thoughts are you?" he asked with a smile.

Alec didn't even answer that. He rolled his eyes. "It's not melancholy. It's just... I don't know what it is. I just want another twelve hundred years with him, or twelve thousand. I didn't ask for these powers, and if given the chance, I'd give them away."

"Why?"

"Because of the risk they pose to him, to you, and Jodis."

He shook his head. "Risk? You mean awesome adventures. There hasn't been a dull moment since the day we met you."

"Gee, thanks."

Eiji grinned. "You're most welcome."

Alec laughed quietly. "I still owe you driving lessons. Don't think I've forgotten."

"How about we wait until Cronin stops having connniptions every time you leave the house?"

Alec snorted. "I know it's tradition to be late, but speaking of leaving...."

Eiji grinned. "I've kept you here long enough. He'll start to think we're up to no good if we don't get there soon."

Alec reached out and touched Eiji's arm, closed his eyes and thought of Cronin. Alec didn't need to think of a place to leap, if he didn't want. He could think of a person and turn up to wherever they were. He could also leap another person without touching them, with or without their consent. If he wanted to, he could have leapt Eiji to the middle of the Pacific Ocean. Not that he would. He threatened it once, but that was only because he'd lost to him at backgammon. That might have also been the sofa burning incident, but at least it didn't involve someone being thrown onto another continent without their consent.

Cronin had made him promise he would never do such a thing.

Cronin.

Cronin....

Alec leapt to where Cronin was.

And that just happened to be in the middle of the Calanais Stones in Scotland. There was a gathering of their closest friends. Alec saw Kennard first, Jacques, Jorge and Adelmo, even Bes from Egypt, and Eleanor who had become a close companion to his father, Kole. They'd been inseparable over the last six months, and this made Alec very happy. And Jodis stood at the top of the circle and held her hand out for Eiji.

It was midnight, the stones were illuminated by the stars, and the moon shone a spotlight on the red-haired vampire who stood in the middle. And what Alec saw took his breath away. Cronin was waiting in the center of the circle, dressed impeccably in a kilt, white shirt, black barathea jacket, and traditional brogues.

Alec had no clue he was going to wear a kilt. They'd

talked about suits, organized suits, even bought and paid for *suits*.

Yet there he stood wearing a kilt.

Alec blinked back tears as he walked into the center of the stones to meet him. How he'd managed to keep this a secret, Alec could only guess. "A kilt?"

"Traditional tartan," he said.

Alec took a deep breath and exhaled slowly. "You better be real traditional underneath that kilt."

Everyone laughed and Cronin blushed.

Kole stepped into the circle then, to officiate. It was Cronin who asked Kole for his blessing to wed his son, but he also asked if he'd like to perform this ceremony. Cronin had said it would mean more if Alec's father would be the one to see them wed. Kole cried and hugged Cronin a lot, but of course he said yes.

Kole held his hand out to Cronin first. "Your sash?"

Alec walked behind Cronin and took Cronin's jacket off for him, and waited for Cronin to unpin the tartan sash. When he'd handed the long strip of red tartan to Kole, Alec helped Cronin back into the tight fitting jacket and slowly, savoring every second, walked back to face Cronin.

They each held out their right hand, and Kole wrapped the sash around their wrists and ceremoniously tied the material in a knot. And Alec saw what it was. Red plaid, wrapped around their hands. What Jorge had said all along was right. 'When the red hand holds the key, forever is in the stones.'

Alec and Cronin both turned in unison to look at Jorge, and the little boy bounced on his toes and clapped his hands.

"Jorge saw it. Jorge saw it."

Adelmo put his hand on the boy's shoulder, shushing him like a father would a son, and everyone laughed.

Eventually, Kole cleared his throat, getting back to the ceremony.

"Upon this day, your hands we bind,

A symbol of your hearts entwined.

To witness this, we ask of thee,

Your union forever blessed be."

Cronin grinned and leaned in to kiss Alec quickly. He was just beaming happiness, and everyone who looked on smiled at his obvious joy. He unwrapped his and Alec's hand, then in what was a traditional show of the joining of clans, with a bowed head, he offered his tartan sash to Alec.

Alec's eyes welled with tears as he took the plaid cloth. "I am honored to be your husband."

Cronin took hold of Alec's face and kissed him, interrupted again by Kole clearing his throat. Alec looked to his dad to see that he was holding a folded cloth. Not just any cloth. The MacAidan tartan. Alec took the small piece of old material, no bigger than a handkerchief, and holding it out to Cronin, he bowed his head.

Cronin took the offering and put it to his heart. "I am honored to be your husband. To stand here where your new life began," Cronin said reverently.

"And so it begins here again with you now," Alec finished. "Forever by fate, wed by choice."

Cronin's eyes filled with tears. "I would choose you."

Alec leaned in and kissed him softly. "And I would choose you."

~*The End*

ABOUT THE AUTHOR

N.R. Walker is an Australian author, who loves her genre of gay romance. She loves writing and spends far too much time doing it, but wouldn't have it any other way.

She is many things: a mother, a wife, a sister, a writer. She has pretty, pretty boys who live in her head, who don't let her sleep at night unless she gives them life with words.

She likes it when they do dirty, dirty things... but likes it even more when they fall in love.

She used to think having people in her head talking to her was weird, until one day she happened across other writers who told her it was normal.

She's been writing ever since...

ALSO BY N.R. WALKER

The Spencer Cohen Series, Book One

The Spencer Cohen Series, Book Two

The Spencer Cohen Series, Book Three

The Spencer Cohen Series, Yanni's Story

Blood & Milk

The Weight Of It All

A Very Henry Christmas (The Weight of It All 1.5)

Perfect Catch

Switched

Imago

Imagines

Red Dirt Heart Imago

On Davis Row

Finders Keepers

Evolved

Galaxies and Oceans

Private Charter

Nova Praetorian

A Soldier's Wish

Upside Down

The Hate You Drink

Sir

Titles in Audio:

Cronin's Key

Free Reads:

Sixty Five Hours
Learning to Feel
His Grandfather's Watch (And The Story of Billy and Hale)
The Twelfth of Never (Blind Faith 3.5)
Twelve Days of Christmas (Sixty Five Hours Christmas)
Best of Both Worlds

Translated Titles:

Fiducia Cieca (Italian translation of Blind Faith)
Attraverso Questi Occhi (Italian translation of Through These Eyes)
Preso alla Sprovvista (Italian translation of Blindside)
Il giorno del Mai (Italian translation of Blind Faith 3.5)
Cuore di Terra Rossa (Italian translation of Red Dirt Heart)
Cuore di Terra Rossa 2 (Italian translation of Red Dirt Heart 2)
Cuore di Terra Rossa 3 (Italian translation of Red Dirt Heart 3)
Cuore di Terra Rossa 4 (Italian translation of Red Dirt Heart 4)
Natale di terra rossa (Red dirt Christmas)
Intervento di Retrofit (Italian translation of Elements of Retrofit)
A Chiare Linee (Italian translation of Clarity of Lines)
Spencer Cohen 1 Serie: Spencer Cohen
Spencer Cohen 2 Serie: Spencer Cohen
Spencer Cohen 3 Serie: Spencer Cohen

Punto di non Ritorno (Italian translation of Point of No Return)

Punto di Rottura (Italian translation of Breaking Point)

Confiance Aveugle (French translation of Blind Faith)

A travers ces yeux: Confiance Aveugle 2 (French translation of Through These Eyes)

Aveugle: Confiance Aveugle 3 (French translation of Blindside)

À Jamais (French translation of Blind Faith 3.5)

Cronin's Key (French translation)

Cronin's Key II (French translation)

Au Coeur de Sutton Station (French translation of Red Dirt Heart)

Partir ou rester (French translation of Red Dirt Heart 2)

Faire Face (French translation of Red Dirt Heart 3)

Trouver sa Place (French translation of Red Dirt Heart 4)

Rote Erde (German translation of Red Dirt Heart)

Rote Erde 2 (German translation of Red Dirt Heart 2)

Sixty Five Hours (Thai translation)

Finders Keepers (Thai translation)

Made in the USA
Monee, IL
07 July 2024

61311603R00142